...and the kids:

A Disorientation Guide for the College-Bound

by Kyle Bern

authorHOUSE®

AuthorHouse™
1663 Liberty Drive
Bloomington, IN 47403
www.authorhouse.com
Phone: 1-800-839-8640

First published by AuthorHouse 05/12/2011

ISBN: 978-1-4567-5300-9 (e)
ISBN: 978-1-4567-5301-6 (sc)

Library of Congress Control Number: 2011903911

Printed in the United States of America

Disclaimer: This is a work of fiction. All of the characters, incidents, and dialogue are imaginary and are not intended to refer to any living persons.

Comfort me
Cover me
                    Deerhunter

1.

My leg is on fire.

This seems like it should hurt but it doesn't, at least not now. Still, I know this situation is abnormal and I should do something about it, so I look away from the flames slowly creeping up the right leg of my jeans and say, "Steve."

Steve is sitting at the kitchen table and staring at something and he's been there forever but when I say his name he jumps up and rushes over to me saying, "Shit."

"Get the fuck down. Get on the floor," Steve is saying, so I do that. I'm lying on the floor and Steve is stomping on my leg and even though my heart is racing, something's inside me telling me that there is danger, I just can't bring my conscious mind to recognize it.

Steve continues stomping on my leg and then he's rolling me around on the floor and shouting for Brian to bring him a blanket, and suddenly the pain registers. My leg is searing and throbbing, from the flames or Steve's feet I don't know, but something inside is pushing and slamming itself against it so hard I start wailing, or maybe I'm giggling, I don't really know the difference now. The pain in my leg is the focal point of existence, the only feeling that ever has or ever will matter, and even though I'm still screaming and gurgling incomprehensible things I'm oddly unafraid. All I can really *think* is, This would be a funny way to die. All I can really *feel* is the pain in my leg and it needs to come out some how, so it does in my garbled shouts. I guess I'm kind of hysterical.

By this point Brian has covered my leg with a blanket and I guess the flames are out because Steve is standing back, panting, saying Holy shit, over and over again. I'm still screaming and giggling though, saying Steve, Steve, and then I'm rolling around on the floor and I can't stop laughing and screaming until Steve grabs me by the shoulders and says, Shut the fuck up, into my face, so I do and I hug him hard. He doesn't resist, just lets me embrace him, and then he hugs me back.

"Do not fucking use the stove when you are on heroin. Ever again." Steve is staring into my eyes when he says this and he seems so serious that I nod, promising I never will. I look over to the stove where I was trying to boil milk for some reason, and the milk has green things in it (grass, I realize dimly) where it's plastered against the stove and dripping down onto the floor. Steve walks over to the stove and turns the flame off.

"You're going to have to clean this up," he says, and I nod again, but his words are meaningless to me. Again there is only this moment, past present and future converged into one. We've been in this kitchen forever, and we will be here forever. This fate of ours is absurd, yes, and somewhere there is a twang of amusement at it, almost regret, but I know instinctively and fully that any regret is pointless. This is the way things always have been, and there is no other way. It is as pointless to question it as it is to question the existence of the sun or the earth beneath our feet. I am sitting in the middle of the kitchen floor, and I have always been here.

❧

The right leg of my pants is blackened and frayed and there are holes in some places where charred skin is visible and I can feel where the hairs were burned off, but it looks cool as hell, a kind of battle scar, and it reminds me of what someone once said about how if you get blood on something its punk rock factor instantly goes up at least thirty percent, so I decide to keep the pants on when I go outside to smoke a cigarette. As I step out into the hall, I notice all the doors are closed, and voices are audible within some of the rooms, but right now this all carries negative significance so I simply float down the hall to the elevator. Time has started to break apart again and rather than the weighted fatality of everything each moment now seems completely meaningless, and this is exhilarating so when I press the down button for the elevator, waiting for the elevator to arrive, I pace the hall, jump up and touch the ceiling, giggle, feel my own momentum, play with the lighter in my pocket.

The elevator is here. I get inside and push the button for the lobby. I'm floating. The elevator stops on the sixth floor and some people get in and sneer at me. I'm sort of amazed by how completely this does not affect me. The elevator doors open. I'm walking through the lobby. People are staring at me. I pass the security guard. I push open the door to the vestibule and then the door that leads outside. Outside people are sitting on the stoop or standing around. Most of them are staring at me. I don't care. I walk a little bit and then light a cigarette, spinning and staring at the sky.

I'm sick of this. I want something to happen, so I throw

3

the cigarette away and go inside. I'll probably smoke grass before bed. I wonder what tomorrow will be like.

I walk back inside and as I'm waiting for the elevator to go back up an R.A. walks up to me from I don't know where. I smile at her; she doesn't smile back. She's looking at my pants. I guess I need to offer some explanation but I'm too dazed to think of anything so I just say, Hey, what's up. The R.A. doesn't say anything so I stare at the numbers going down: 7...6...5... I really want the elevator to get here. Suddenly the R.A. says, Are you okay? I look at her. The expression on her face is indiscernible.

"Oh yeah, I'm fine. I just...did some stuff tonight," I say, and giggle. She continues staring and I continue to be unable to read her expression and then she says, "But you're okay, right?"

"Oh yeah, I'm fine," I repeat, and she nods. This conversation appears to be over and I am relieved. The elevator is here. I step inside and so does the R.A. She gets out on the seventh floor and tells me to have a good night. I smile and thank her. I really want to smoke some grass.

I get out on the eleventh floor and walk to my suite. Inside is empty and I guess everyone is asleep. I go into my bedroom and see my roommate, Tim, sitting on the bed across the room from mine, doing something on his laptop. He looks up and says, you're fucking pathetic, and then he sneers. I shrug. I roll a joint. I open the window and light the joint. After two puffs I offer it to Tim, who shakes his head. I continue smoking it. I'm starting to calm down, which means the dread is starting to creep back into me. Whatever. This will all make sense tomorrow, probably.

2.

I'm awake but I don't want to be, so I keep my eyes closed.

My leg hurts. I listen. My roommate, Tim, is rustling through some papers, and he shouts to Brian that he needs a paintbrush back. The door to the kitchen is open. Brian shouts back that he needs the brush for intricate strokes on his whale's vagina, and it needs to be exact because it's a metaphor for something I can't hear because someone, presumably Steve, slams a cabinet door.

"What the fuck," Steve is saying, and I'm keeping my eyes closed but listening very attentively now as, I guess, Steve opens the refrigerator door, takes out a heavy object, and slams it on the table. He then picks the object up and I hear him drinking frantically, choking down water like a crazed animal, before he slams the object down again.

"When no one cleans their glasses, I drink from the water filter," Steve says, in a casual tone that isn't supposed to hide the true anger beneath it, and then there is a pause. "I told him to clean the fucking stove," Steve says, and I open my eyes.

Where I am is in my bed and the lights are off but it's bright anyway because sun is streaming in through the window and the blinds are drawn but the slats are open, and my roommate is sitting at the desk at the foot of his bed and there are paintings, and cardboard models, and experimental sculptures, and other art projects he's done strewn across the surface of his desk, and I look over to my desk and see that my laptop, a white one, a Mac, is covered in ash, and Steve is still screaming from the kitchen.

I sit up and my left leg feels like someone stampeded over it and my head hurts and I feel vaguely nauseous, but I swing my legs over the side of my bed anyway, preparing to get down.

"Hey," I say to my roommate, and he looks up from his desk and says, "Hey man," and he's grinning. I don't want to think about why this might be and I suddenly need to go to the bathroom very badly so I stumble through our bedroom door, which has a huge drawing that my roommate did of a marijuana leaf decorated in Christmas ornaments with the words "Merry X-Mas" written above it taped to its outside, into the kitchen where Steve is now standing and staring at me, so I swagger right, towards the bathroom, seeing Brian sitting at the kitchen table, where I nod to him, say "Hey dude," and there's a painting of some kind of aquatic landscape on the table in front of him, which he looks up from to say, "Hey," and then after a pause, "good morning," and I continue moving towards the bathroom until I can see my reflection in the mirror and I shut the door behind me.

My reflection in the mirror in not unrevolting and I look away hastily, meanwhile listening to hear Steve clear his throat and shout to say, "Tad?"

I'm frozen, but the pain in my stomach becomes vivid so I hit the toilet and, regaining my composure, shout back, "Yeah?"

"Are you planning to clean up the stove?"

Steve says this in the most sarcastic tone possible and I immediately start shitting, emptying the contents of my bowels into the toilet, a zen moment which is interrupted by the nagging fear at the back of my skull and I muster a "Yeah dude, sorry."

Steve sighs so loudly I can hear it, and then I hear him walk into his bedroom. I sigh, slumping on the toilet seat, relieved, and I begin to roll some toilet paper around my hand.

❧

Back outside I'm feeling better but still somewhat sick and with a dull headache and I know I'm going to need some Motrin and some grass before I do anything else. I walk back into my room and sit down at my desk. My roommate is sitting at his desk, and he's drawing something with pencils. I grab a Motrin from the lidless canister on my desk and swallow it with a gulp of the SmartWater that's also on my desk. I study the white laptop in front of me, wondering where these ashes came from. I don't think I smoked from a piece last night, but maybe I did. Even if I did, though, it wouldn't have produced nearly this much ash. I decide to just shake the ashes onto the floor, and then I put the laptop back on my desk, open it, and while it's starting up I take my piece and a bag of grass from the shelf above me. I break apart pieces of grass and pack them into the bowl. The Welcome screen appears and I log in. I continue packing grass into the bowl, and it seems to be taking me a while, but finally I finish and then I open Safari and check my school email account before I walk to the window with the piece in my hand, grabbing a lighter off my roommate's desk.

"I'll have some of that," my roommate says, looking

up from his drawing, and I nod and say, "Sure." I'm now standing in such a way that my ass is touching the arm of my roommate's chair; so cramped are our living quarters that you can't stand by the window without some part of you touching my roommate's bed or desk, situated on either side of it. My bed and desk are situated in the same way on the opposite side of the room (a roughly six foot walk) only they border the door rather than the window. There is a small shag carpet at the foot of my roommate's bed and there are cowboy boots on top of it. I look away and stare out the window, which I also exhale smoke through. I cough. I look over at my roommate, who's working on his drawing again (of what appears to be some kind of ship) and I say, "Dude."

My roommate looks up and smiles at me. I smile and look away. He stands up from his desk and takes the piece, as well as the lighter, from my hands. My roommate's crotch is now pressed against mine but he quickly turns away, to my relief. My crotch is now touching his ass, though, and as he takes a hit off my bowl I wonder if I should maintain eye contact with him or avoid it entirely. I don't have to make that decision though because my roommate shoves the paraphernalia into my hands and then sits on the foot of his bed. I feel something like disappointment; but the grass is now in my hands, as well as the means to smoke it, so I press a finger against the carb, hold the flame to the bowl, and take another hit. I hold my breath. I look over at my roommate, who is now doing something on his laptop, a white one, a Mac, like mine, and then I look out the window again because my lungs are starting to burn and I see the gigantic Levi's advertisement plastered to the wall of the parking garage across the street before I exhale hard and cough. I shut my eyes and keep coughing. Sun is streaming through the window, a late fall day, and I can feel warmth on my face and see red beneath my eyelids. It reminds me of something and I stop coughing. I open my eyes. My roommate is staring at me, and then at the piece in my hand, which is still smoking slightly, and smoke hangs in the air above us.

"We should turn the fan on," my roommate says, and I say, "Yeah," and when he doesn't get up I hand him the piece wordlessly and bend down to take the fan from under his desk. It's a small fan that I bought at a Surprise! Surprise! around the corner from us and which cost forty dollars, which my roommate says is way too much for a fan of that size and caliber and I guess I agree with him. It's already plugged in so I stand up and place it on the edge of his desk, and I face it towards the window before turning it on. My roommate is blowing smoke out the window. The sun is shining brightly, and I have to squint. My roommate hands me the piece and I don't know what happened to my lighter so I take a white lighter from his desk and I light the bowl, inhaling. The smoke is harsh and the sun and the smoke in the air are making me squint and I'm trying to hold my breath but already my lungs are burning, so I look out the window at the 120 foot tall Levi's guy, a buff model leaning against a Cadillac and staring at us with a vaguely menacing expression, and I cough and smoke goes everywhere. I pick up the fan, still coughing, and aim it at the smoke to try to blow it out the window, and my roommate is watching me do this and he says, "It's fine," blankly, and then goes back to looking at his laptop. I'm confused by his apparent agitation so I put the fan back down on the desk. The sun is really bright in here and I'm starting to feel really hot.

"Dude, it's really hot in here," I tell my roommate, and he looks up from his laptop and says, "Yeah, it is pretty hot," in a voice that sounds genuine. My heart is beating very fast now and I lean against the window sill, close my eyes and take deep breaths. I go over the basics, the way someone once told me to: I'm Tad. I'm 18, I go to the Four Brothers art school in Manhattan, I'm from New Jersey. I'm here, now, living with my roommate and two other guys, and even though I'd rather be with Sam, the moment is okay, good enough, something I can handle. I open my eyes again, and I gasp softly. "I think I'm finished," I tell my roommate, and he looks up and half-whines, "Yeah, me too…I'm pretty high." I am too, and although that brief refresher course helped there are still certain things troubling me; foremost, what happened to me last night.

I know it was my first time trying heroin. I had bought a $15 bag of what I thought was grass off two people, a man and a woman, black, a couple maybe, who, it was later obvious, were fried out of their minds on the very drugs they were selling, on the front steps of my dorm building, and when I opened up the little baggie and saw black flakes and powder, Steve confirmed what it was – black tar heroin, he'd done it tons of times before, totally safe if you smoke it as a one-time thing, and besides we'd talked about getting some heroin anyway, so we loaded my piece with the stuff and lit up.

I blink the memories away, which isn't easy because the jeans I had on last night, black and eaten by flame, lay crumpled at the foot of my bed, along with the pointy blue '80s dress shoes I bought at Trash and the frilly colonial-looking button-down I bought at Metropolis. The more I look at the jeans, though, the better the night seems; the excitement, the thrill, the rebellion; until all that's left is a warm feeling of how crazy it all was. Satisfied, I begin to walk to the kitchen. What I really want to do is turn on my roommate's high-definition LCD TV and watch something funny, maybe South Park, but I remember none of us have it on DVD, and anyway what I actually really want to do is call Sam, but I know that isn't an option right now. So I continue past the TV, which sits atop a DVD player on a shelf high above the two desks and is by far the most expensive furnishing in the place, except maybe our laptops, and walk into the kitchen. I have my cellphone in my pocket, and I touch it with my hand just to make sure, in case Sam calls, or, more likely, texts me. The kitchen is less bright than the bedroom and the timeless haze of the fluorescent light that hangs in the air is somewhat comforting to me. I begin to think about myself, the easiest way to stay positive, as I walk across the grimy flat tiled floor from my bedroom to the sink, passing a now empty table with four chairs skewed around it, looking to the left as I pass a blank wall and then seeing that my suitemates, Steve and Brian, have left their door slightly open, and I look away calmly, noticing the microwave which should be on the table but for some reason is now on the floor, by the foot of the sink, where I now arrive. Next to the sink is a stove that's covered in a semi-dried white foam with traces of yellow and brown, and there are big green globs in the foam. Some of the foam has dripped down the oven door and dried there, leaving a line like a slug, speckled in green and brown. The realization that this is what remains of the milk and grass I boiled last night conjures up the memory of the smell, which I might, in fact, be smelling right now, if I weren't high. As I look into the sink and notice the big metal pot plastered with this foamy substance, I'm glad I'm high. I turn on the water and pour some of Brian's organic, biodegradable soap into the pot, and I pick up a dried orange sponge and begin to scrub. I'm washing this white foamy shit out of the pot, which is thankfully easy to get off, but I can't stop looking to the side, staring at the white stove with its circular black flame things and the white muck, bubbly in places, brown with traces of dirt from the stove beneath it, and the huge gobs of grass, stuck there, and immediately I gag. I can't help it. I put a hand over my mouth. No one seems to notice. I turn to my left and walk the few feet to the refrigerator, which is against the wall and the to the right of the door to my suitemates' bedroom, and I take out the water filter but noticing it's empty I slide it back in and shut the refrigerator door before sprinting back to the sink, looking frantically now for a cup in the cabinet above it, only finding a shot glass but I'd rather not drink straight from the faucet so I turn the faucet on and fill the glass with cold water, gulping it down quickly. I fill the glass again and drink, more slowly this time, because I'm feeling better. To be safe I go over the basics, just standing there in the kitchen, looking across the room at my reflection in the narrow floor-to-ceiling mirror, which is to the right of the bathroom door, which is open but the lights are off so I can't really see my reflection in the mirror above the bathroom sink: I went to Vassar. I wanted to major in writing, but I got kicked out. I came to Manhattan for the fall semester at Four Brothers, my safety school. I want to be a visual artist. In some ways Four Brothers is different from Vassar but in more ways it's very, very similar. I'm not sure what my major will be yet; perhaps illustration. What I'd really like to do is be a writing major, but I already know I wouldn't be any good at that. More than any of this, though, I'm interested in Sam.

I blush and look away from the mirror, not sure why I said that. I take my cellphone out of my pocket, checking it just in case Sam has called or texted me and I missed it. When I see he hasn't I put my cellphone back in my pocket, return to the sink, rinse my glass, and continue scrubbing.

3.

Sam wakes up to Meet The Press and tells his roommate, Jason, to lower that shit. He's trying to remember what he did last night but his mind is looping on a guy who puked on the subway and made everyone laugh. That makes Sam feel good, and then it makes him feel sad. He yawns, scratches his crotch, rolls over, buries his face in his pillow, knowing he won't fall back asleep now but not wanting to open his eyes for some reason. When he does he looks across the room and sees Jason—pale, thin, and with a crew cut that makes him look like a shell shocked war veteran or a junkie or both—sitting on his bed, eyes wide, watching Meet The Press. There's a timer on the bottom of the screen counting down the days, hours, and minutes until the election. Sam watches it for some time, listening to the talking heads talk about the inevitability of an Obama victory, which makes him feel good, and then he gets out of bed. He pulls the jeans on the floor on over his frail hips, which are one of his own favorite physical attributes, and whips out his cellphone from a pocket. The envelope icon which tells him he has new texts makes him feel good because it makes him feel needed, and when he sees it's just a text from Kay and not from Tad his heart sinks, to use a stupid cliché. Kay wants him to meet her at her dorm. She doesn't say why. She's kind of crazy so Sam doesn't waste time trying to figure it out. Instead he scans his memory banks of the night before as the noise from the TV sort of evaporates. He remembers doing shots of Jagermeister with Jason and then leaving his room, meeting up with Rebecca, Autumn, and George, swallowing three hits of ecstasy, the subway ride to Brooklyn where he saw that guy throw up, which is haunting him vaguely, for some reason, feeling fat in his glam rocker costume, and then…Shit, where is that costume? Sam scans the floor, his desk, his bed, even opens his wardrobe just in case. He doesn't actually give a shit about the costume, even though it cost him over a hundred bucks, he just wants to see it because maybe it will offer some insight into what happened to him last night. Did he even have it when he got back here? He woke up in briefs and a t-shirt, so he can't be sure. He even deigns to ask Jason if he's seen a huge blonde wig or sparkly platform boots or leather pants anywhere and Jason, predictably, doesn't look away from the TV when he whispers, barely audible, "No, man." Shit. Now Sam wants to know what his hair looks like so he walks out of the small double room he shares with Jason, which looks exactly like the room Tad and Tim share only it's not connected to a suite, into the hallway to find an empty bathroom, lock the door, and check himself out in the mirror. His usually straight down blonde hair is all twisted and knotted for some reason and now he can tell that he smells pretty bad and then he hears screaming coming from somewhere which unnerves him, for some reason. He looks down and sees that even though he's gripping the sink so hard his knuckles are white his hands are shaking anyway. That's so weird that he's just going to take a shower and then, yeah, head over to Kay's, so he walks back to his room, grabs a towel from the floor and a bottle of St. Ives Body Wash from inside his open wardrobe, and walks back to the bathroom. He unbuttons, unzips his jeans, pulls off his t-shirt, kicks off the Vans sneakers he didn't even realize he was wearing until now, pulls off his boxers, and steps into the shower naked. He turns on the water and cowers in one corner while he waits for it to heat up. While this happening he's studying the bottle of body wash, which contains Energizing Citrus that will Awaken Your Senses. Sam grunts, which indicates some mix of satisfaction and placidity, and squeezes the opaque green gel with tiny beads in it into a palm and then rubs that gel all over his chest, lathering it into white foam over his torso and pubic hair, and then Sam steps into the stream of water because he can tell by the drops of water that are splashing him that it's hot enough.

Last night, while Sam was throwing up in Death By Audio's miniscule bathroom and Tad was freaking out on heroin, Jason was lying on his bed, pleasantly wasted, watching CNN. That's what he's doing now, only he's not really wasted, just zonked out on Seroquel. Someone on TV says something about Barack Obama. Someone else says something about Sarah Palin. A woman mentions John McCain and then a recession that might turn into a depression. Someone says something about Barack Obama. Someone else says something about McCain, then about Henry Kissinger. Then someone says something about George W. Bush. Then someone says something about General Petraeus. Then everyone is talking about Obama. Jason doesn't really hear or see this; sound and light passes over him in patterns, and those patterns trigger recognition in his brain. Who gives a shit. Eventually Sam walks back into the room wearing only a towel and Jason barely has to try not to snap his eyes directly to Sam's crotch. That's how he knows the medication is helping with his paranoia: Sam can be here, half naked, and Jason's eyes barely leave the screen. Jason sinks lower into his bed as Sam pulls some boxers on under the towel and then takes the towel off, pulls on some jeans, smears deodorant in his armpits and then pulls on a t-shirt. Jason's head has been sort of vibrating this whole time, but when Sam pulls on a tight denim jacket it stops. Jason hates himself for a few minutes because he couldn't stop himself from shaking but the Seroquel quickly blots that feeling out, the drug acting as a cloud in his brain. Sam leaves the room and Jason is able to concentrate fully on the TV again.

Sam is walking down the hall to the elevator because he needs to meet Kay and find out what the fuck is up with her now. He rides the elevator down to the lobby and leaves the building. He makes a left, onto Sixth Street, walking toward Third Avenue, and when he gets to Third Avenue he makes another left to walk the six streets up to Kay's dorm at Twelfth Street and Third Avenue. When Sam gets there he doesn't need to call or text Kay because she's already standing outside and she doesn't look good. Her face is covered in what looks like a thin white paste, and Sam thinks this is weird but it doesn't stop him from smiling and saying, "Hey, what's up?" Kay doesn't smile, just looks back at him, that white stuff covering her skin, which Sam now sees is pockmarked and actually torn up in places, and Kay says, "I was late for class yesterday." Sam, still smiling, says, "Don't worry about it, I'm late all the time," and now his eyes are darting from Kay's paper-white face to the door of her dorm to the people sitting outside her dorm to down the street to the left and then down the street to the right, becoming increasingly uncomfortable, and that's when Kay's lip starts to tremble and she says, her voice shaking, "No, you don't understand," and she turns from Sam and walks down the street fast. Sam watches her go and then looks around for someone who might have witnessed this weird fucking scene, to help him make sense of it or at least agree with him that this girl was acting really, really weird, and although that's nothing new for Kay the white paste and the torn up skin make Sam feel uncomfortable so when he starts walking back to his dorm he decides he needs to pick up some weed and get high.

❧

When Sam gets back to his dorm Jason is still watching CNN. Sam asks Jason if he wants to get high. Jason, not a pot fan but wanting to be fucked up, says yes tentatively. Sam takes out his cellphone and just as he's about to call one of his dealers he notices he has a new text from Tad and smiles. The text says: "Hey, what are you doing tonight? Wanna hang out?" Sam doesn't reply, thinking he'll deal with it later, instead selecting the number of a weed delivery service from his contact list and pressing send. The same guy who always answers answers and Sam says it's him and then tells the guy he needs a fifty. A dime bag would be fine but these guys only sell 50 or 60 dollar bags of weed. An hour passes during which Sam does stuff on the internet, then the guy calls him. Sam leaves his dorm, gives fifty dollars to the dealer, and gets the weed. He smokes it with Jason. Afterward Jason lays on his bed, flips the TV to CNN, and stares. Sam just watches Jason for five, ten, fifteen minutes, totally confused about where the kid is, mentally, and then he goes outside to smoke a cigarette.

When Sam is outside he runs into George, which is perfect, because he's still been trying to figure out what he did last night. George tells Sam that Sam got totally wasted at Death By Audio, puked four different times, twice all over his clothes, and then George and Rebecca, but not Autumn because she had a limp from stepping on a cracked glass which some drunk cunt had thrown at her while she was running around Death By Audio without shoes on, had to carry him by his shoulders to the subway, sit him down, talk him out of puking on the ride back to his dorm, and then guide him upstairs to his bed, his body limp and eyes drooping closed, open, closed, open, the whole time.

Sam listens to all this in silence, nodding at appropriate times while he smokes his cigarette, turning his head to exhale so he doesn't blow smoke in George's face.

Sam asks, "So, uh, what are Rebecca and Autumn doing now?"

George says, "Rebecca is at Crunch. I haven't heard from Autumn today."

Sam nods. George finished the cigarette he was smoking when Sam came outside about three sentences ago and neither Sam nor George say anything while Sam finishes his. Soon Sam does, and he throws the butt on the ground.

Sam says, "I'll see you around, man."

George says, "Later, man."

Sam walks back inside. For some reason George doesn't.

Sam gets back to his room and he's feeling a combination of unpleasant feelings but can't think of the words for any of them and he really just wants to watch a movie, something funny, but there's Jason, lying on his bed, watching CNN, but Sam can't be here like this so he says to Jason, "Hey man, wanna watch The Simpsons?"

Jason turns his head slightly, eyeballing Sam and then quickly stopping himself, and even though he feels really nervous about doing something with Sam he feels even more excited so he says, "Sure, man."

Sam's stretching out on his bed now, trying to get

comfortable. Jason picks up the remote and switches the channel to FOX but instead of The Simpsons it's just more news. Jason and Sam stare at the screen in silence.

❧

Later that night Sam is in Autumn's room. Sam just texted Tad saying he can't hang out tonight, sorry. Sam and Autumn are watching Lifetime on Autumn's small color TV, not LCD, which makes Sam sort of roll his eyes internally. The show they're watching is some home makeover show.

Sam says, "Project Runway is tomorrow, right?"

Autumn says, "Yeah."

They're high, and a guy on TV is talking about wood finishing. Then the guy on TV says stuff about tabletops and marble versus granite.

Before this, Sam and Autumn smoked a joint down the block, so they're both pretty high. After this, Sam will go back to his room, try to read Genesis for his Religion and Myth class, stop after being unable to concentrate, and go to sleep. That's all you really need to know.

The election is in three days.

4.

Sam wakes up with two texts. One is from Tad and says, "hey man!" The other is from Kay and says, "we should meet for breakfast/lunch." The text from Tad makes Sam feel happy; the one from Kay, ambivalent. He is pretty hungry though, so, brushing hair from his eyes, he types in "sure. where do you want to eat?" on his cellphone and sends it to Kay. Jason is asleep. The TV is off. Sam feels vaguely relieved. He grabs a towel, his small black bag of toiletry which looks like a bag junkies use to store their heroin and works in and he thinks that's pretty funny, his bottle of St. Ives Body Wash, and then he walks out of the room, down the hall, into a bathroom to take a shower. While he's showering Sam is massaging Body Wash into his scalp and feeling the grainy dead skin on his scalp with the tips of his fingers and it feels good to be washing it out. When Sam gets out of the shower he looks at himself in the mirror, dries his body with a towel, brushes he teeth, rinses toothpaste out of his mouth, dresses, and walks back to his room.

Jason is awake and CNN is on. Keith Olbermann is saying something about either Barack Obama or John

McCain, Sam doesn't know which. Sam takes his cellphone out of his jeans pocket and reads the new text from Kay: "the diner on second ave." Sam replies, "rad meet you there in 45 min?," not expecting a response. As Sam is about to leave the room Jason stops him by saying, "Hey man, is there any Jager left?" Sam says, "I don't think so. You can check the fridge." Jason says, "Thanks." Speaking of the fridge, Sam walks through the kitchen on his way out the door and down the hall and to the elevator and down to the lobby and out of the building to meet Kay at the diner on Second Avenue.

When Sam arrives Kay is there already. Big surprise. Sam watches her through the window before going inside. She's sitting at the counter, staring down at a cup of something. There's a spoon in the cup. Waiters walk around behind the counter, taking orders from people sitting in front of the counter, dropping dishes off on top of the counter. Kay looks alarmingly thin, but when doesn't she? Sam enters the diner.

He sits on a stool next to her and grabs a menu from a stack to the left of a display case of muffins. He scans the breakfast column, deciding what we wants to eat. He decides on french toast, sticks his hand up in the air to signal a waiter's attention, tells the waiter he wants french toast, and then turns to Kay and says, "Hey. What's up?"

Kay is still looking into the cup (coffee, Sam observes, glancing over) but when Sam speaks to her she looks at him and smiles, though it looks kind of grim, and she says "Not much, Sam. How are you?"

Sam says, "I'm fine," and then after a pause, "how are you?" Sam is watching the diner's employees walk around behind the counter when Kay says, "I'm okay. Sorry about freaking out the other day." Sam says, "It's okay," and then after a pause, "don't worry about it."

"I'm such a fuck up," Kay says. "You're not," Sam says, but he's already getting bored of this so he's scanning the diner with his eyes, trying to get a waiter's attention so he can get some of the delicious challah bread they serve here.

"Do you want any of that bread," Sam is saying to Kay when he makes eye contact with a waiter and says, "Hey, can we get some challah bread?" The waiter nods and walks away. Moments later a plastic cup filled with water is slammed down in front of Sam. Sam sighs, grabs a nearby straw, tears the paper off it, puts it in the cup, and drinks. Then he stops drinking. He looks around the diner again, anticipating that bread, and when he doesn't see it coming he looks at Kay again and says, "So do you want any of that bread or not?"

"I'm fine," Kay says, and Sam doesn't say anything. Soon the bread is brought to him on a paper plate, already buttered, and he takes a big bite and chews hungrily before putting the bread back down and saying to Kay, "So, what's up?"

"Nothing," Kay says, sounding irritable now, and Sam is losing patience. Kay stirs her coffee with the spoon, even though it's black, and then takes a sip. Sam looks at Kay's face to see if any of the white stuff is plastered there now and it isn't but he sees scabs and open wounds, not bloody, more like craters where skin has been dug away. Sam thinks about this for a minute, slightly worried, and then he gets his french toast and starts eating.

When Sam finishes eating his french toast and Kay finishes drinking her coffee they pay and leave the diner. Outside, Kay lights an American Spirits cigarette. Sam asks if he can have one and Kay gives him one. Sam thanks her. Sam tells Kay he'll see her later and Kay walks away. Sam takes out his cellphone and calls George.

"I just had lunch with Kay," Sam says to George. "Oh," George sarcastically says, "how was that?" "It was fine," Sam says hastily. "So, uh, what's up?" "Not much man, Autumn and I were just wondering if you wanted to come to this bar in Brooklyn," George says. Sam says, "Isn't it, like, shit... what time is it?"

5.

It's Sunday night and I'm smoking a joint and feeling pretty good. The movie we're watching is *Earth Girls Are Easy*. I exhale and pass to the left. "Does anyone have an ashtray?," someone asks, and my roommate begins rooting around above his desk. The shades are drawn and the lights are off and it's really dark in here. I'm sitting in a chair in the back of the room and there are four or five other people in here, I'm not sure. On screen Jim Carrey is dressed like an alien, covered in orange fur. I'm a little drunk. Steve is sitting in the chair to my left and he's who I passed the joint to but he's not who asked for the ashtray. This seems weird but I ignore it. Got to keep my mind clear. Got to stay in the moment.

I look at Steve's face just as he's beginning to breathe out smoke and I can't see his eyes but he's staring at the TV, motionless. Steve hasn't said anything, I don't think, since we duct taped the door shut. This is so no smoke gets out of the room, and we also taped over the air vent above the door. I look at the TV, where a woman in a bikini is sitting by a pool. Someone is sitting on my bed, to the right of me, and across the room there is also someone sitting on my roommate's bed. My roommate sits at his desk, chair pushed slightly back. Everyone is watching the movie but for some reason I can't concentrate. I need another drink, so I ask the room, "Hey is there, uh, any beer left?" No response. This is making me uncomfortable because I'm not sure if people heard me and are just ignoring me or they actually didn't hear me, so I turn to Steve and say, "Hey man, is there any more beer?" Steve turns to me, looking away from the TV, bright colors all over his face, and he says, "Uh, I don't know," and he makes a sound that implies vague derision as he turns back to the TV. I'm not sure what to do for a moment and then I stand up and walk slowly across the room. On my desk it's hard to see but there's an empty bottle of Romana Sambuca here, as expected, my own bottle which I bought at Fred's Liquors across town, and which I drank all of, usually in mornings before classes, over the course of about four days. There are also two nearly empty Forties on the desk, one mine and one Steve's, and I drink the remains of both. The liquor tastes warm and stale and it's not doing its job. I look to my left, over at my roommate's desk, and I can see, silhouetted, a wine bottle and a few bottles of beer. I try to walk quickly past the TV, but all of a sudden people start laughing and I'm startled, but I quickly regain my composure and stroll rapidly to my roommate's desk. I look down, stepping around my roommate's leg and the leg of his chair, trying to get out of his line of vision as quickly and easily as possible, and make it to the window. The window is open and there's a cool breeze blowing in but an even cooler one blowing out: the fan on my roommate's desk, pointed towards the window. I stand in this air vortex for a while before hastily kneeling down to examine the wine bottle on my roommate's desk (about one-fourth full), the three bottles of beer (all finished), and the bottle of

Absolut Vodka (which I also bought, and there's only a little bit left of it). I face in the general direction of the room and ask, "Does anyone want this wine?" I now see that the person sitting on my bed is Amanda, a neighbor from across the hall, and she's shaking her head no; Steve is facing the TV and gives no indication that he heard me; Kay, my roommate's friend, is lying on my roommate's bed and she says, "No"; my roommate turns to face me, his face and my crotch at roughly the same level, so he looks up and half-whines, "No, you go ahead"; so I do. I'm drinking straight from the bottle and I hope no one sees me, and, trying to stay positive, I doubt anyone does because they are so fixated on the movie. My roommate isn't even looking at me any more, although our feet touch. On screen Jim Carrey and the two other actors dressed as aliens are being shaved by the woman in the bikini and, underneath all that colorful fur, is Jim Carrey and the two other actors with bleached blond hair, looking like surfers. I continue drinking, averting my eyes from the screen, turning to face the window, and it's dark out and I see speckled light in the distance and when I put my face to the window I see the light is just other windows, like I knew it would be, on the building across the street, and I hope no one from that building is looking in here now.

The wine bottle is empty and I want to call Sam. I haven't talked to him yet today. I place the wine bottle back on my roommate's desk, then I pick up my bottle of vodka and return to my seat with it, trying to step quickly past the glare of the TV. Sitting down, I open the bottle and sniff the vodka, for no real reason, because the jolt of the smell is reassuring in some way, and I take a long sip, staring into the the TV, blues and oranges and reds zipping past me on electrons. On screen, Jim Carrey and the other two actors are walking with the bikini woman in a mall. I watch this movie for about ten seconds as I finish off the vodka and walk carefully out of the room with no explanation. It's difficult to get the door open because it's duct taped shut but I pull hard and a loud tearing sound fills the room, and people start groaning so I quickly step out of the room, into the kitchen, and close the door. The no-time shine of the kitchen is calming, making me feel dull and mechanical but functioning, so I sit down at the table and take my cellphone out of my pocket, to call Sam, and I'm filled instantly with longing but I ignore it, the dull and mechanical necessary now, and the time on my phone says 4:30 am and I am stunned by how late it is, how much time has past, so I check the display on the microwave on the floor and, yes – 4:30 am. Why am I calling Sam, I think, if we have class tomorrow—today, I realize, and I'm cognizant of a faint dread pulsing somewhere distant. Class at 9:30—The Art of the Personal Essay, my one writing class, and the one class Sam and I have together. I decide not to call because I might wake him up and then he would think it's weird that I'm calling so late, and besides he probably won't answer anyway.

I get up from the table and walk to my bedroom door, realizing I should get to bed soon; but, not wanting to kick Amanda off my bed or anyone out of the room on my behalf, I go into the bathroom to brush my teeth, to delay it.

6.

That night Sam is doing lines of Adderall off a copy of *Will You Please Be Quiet, Please?* with George and Autumn.

"Shit," Autumn says. "My foot really hurts. This is good stuff though."

George says, "It's Adderall. How could it not be good stuff."

Sam says, "I like it. This is nice. Do you guys want to go for a walk."

Autumn says, "Yeah." No one moves until Autumn walks across the room and turns on the TV. CNN is on and someone is talking about Barack Obama.

"Turn that shit *off*," Sam says. Jason isn't home and Sam is happy about that. Motherfucker would probably freak out if he saw what they were doing. All Jason does is drink. And watch the news.

"Okay, let's go for a walk," George says, pacing around the dorm room, past the TV and Jason's bed, past Jason's desk, past Sam's desk, past Sam's bed, once, twice, three times.

"How about...Times Square?" Sam asks, and George and Autumn both say, "Sure."

Sam, George, and Autumn leave their dorm at Third Avenue and Sixth Street. On their way uptown they pass convenience stores, drug stores, bars, clubs, none of their names registering in Sam's brain, blurs in the night. When they get to Sixth and Twelfth Sam considers texting Kay, decides against it, and as he's walking past her dorm to Sixth and Thirteenth he becomes aware of the presence of the people he's walking with for the first time since they left because Autumn says, "Shit. I have to go back." George asks, "Why?" Autumn says, "My foot hurts too much. Shit. This really hurts." George sighs and says, "Okay," and they begin to walk back downtown.

When Sam, George, and Autumn get back to the dorms at Third Avenue and Sixth Street they drop Autumn off at her room and then Sam and George go to Sam's room. Jason still isn't home. Sam notices George is trembling, not quite shaking, and doesn't say anything. George says, "Man, this speed is starting to fuck with my head. Do you have anything to take the edge off?" Sam has a prescription to Ativan and offers George some. They each snort three milligrams. George wobbles a little and then says, "Man, that's better. Want to go back out again?"

They get to Twenty-Third Street when George starts saying, "Man, I don't feel so good," and Twenty-Seventh Street when he starts vomiting. George is vomiting in the middle of the sidewalk so Sam guides him, one arm around George's shoulders, to the side of a building. George keeps vomiting. Sam says, "Man. Are you okay?" and then, "I'm sorry, man." When George stops retching he says, "No man, it's my fault. Sorry." Sam says, "It's okay," and they begin walking downtown. Sometimes Sam lets George lean against his shoulder.

When they get back to the dorms Sam and George go to Sam's room. Jason still isn't home. Sam sits on his bed, and then George does. They sit there like that, looking out the window, waiting for the sun to start to rise or maybe just waiting for something to happen. When George falls asleep Sam lays down next to him and then after a few minutes Sam hugs George. This feels good.

7.

Steve, Tim, Tad, Kay, and Amanda are watching *Earth Girls Are Easy*. Brian is in his and Steve's bedroom, reading conspiracy theories on infowars.com. At first Steve is only a little pissed off at Tad. He's more pissed off generally, but thinking about how he has Introduction To Fiction at eight this morning and he'll probably only get an hour of sleep, at most, is focusing his rage on Tad again. Tim is content; he's high, kind of drunk, and watching a funny movie with his friends. Kay is thinking about how she shouldn't have smoked weed. She wants to eat something and she knows she really, really shouldn't have smoked weed. She needs her Adderall fast but unfortunately she doesn't have it with her. The darkness and smallness of this room is becoming really obvious.

Kay is becoming paranoid and her mind is racing out of control and the one thing she absolutely needs right now, on this morning and in her life generally, is control. She looks at Tim but he's looking at the TV, sedated; she looks at Amanda, who is also looking at the TV and is also sedated; she looks at Steve, who has this smirk on his face like he can't relax but still his eyes are fixed on the TV; and then there's Tad, who looks like he's jumping out of his skin, his eyes darting around the room, and she quickly looks away, back at the TV, before she accidentally makes eye contact with the weird asshole. She needs an Adderall; she shouldn't have smoked pot and she needs her fucking Adderall.

Amanda is thinking about the 3D model she hasn't finished and what she's going to tell the instructor of her 3D class tomorrow, but otherwise she's feeling pretty mellow, vibing the weed and the movie.

Brian smoked a little bit of weed and then went into his room. He's reading about the Bilderberg Group on an internet forum. He's reading how a secret meeting in August was when Bilderberg decided to back Obama, and that an Obama victory is inevitable. He's reading about false choice and sham elections and how nothing will change because the handful of worldwide money holders that control the outcome of every election have already stolen Obama and Obama is already a puppet. He's reading all this and taking it all in.

The election is in two days.

8.

The Art of the Personal Essay is where I met Sam.

First day of class, I was pretty stoned and I sat at a desk in the front of the room and it was cold that day and I watched the students walk in—cute blond girl from LA wearing a horrendous North Face jacket, cute jittery Jewish guy from Jersey with a paunch and thick black glasses, wacko art school chick with long black hair who carries a huge canvas around everywhere and she never talks to anyone, except her boyfriend, who seems much more normal, but he isn't in this class and I realized that I don't actually care about any of this, and then Sam.

Sam, his long, dirty-blond hair spectacular in the September light, his pale skin and plump lips and small nose, a baby face, really, so beautiful, and I tried to keep my eyes on him as he walked to his seat, hoping he would understand the implication of my glances and respond to them in some way. He did, eventually; actually, looking back on it, he showed more interest in me than I did in him, at least at first. But I remember watching him, that first day of class, and he kept sneaking glances back at me and then he smiled and then I smiled and I looked away.

After class there were about five of us left, and Sam was there, and we were all talking to the professor about some minor issue, something about advising, but we were really talking to each other about whatever erudite or obscure or interesting observation any of us could think of. I guess we were really just trying to impress each other even back then.

So I'm was going on about something about Hunter S. Thompson and I notice Sam avidly listening, and when I look at him he smiles and then looks away and twirls his finger through his hair. We probably talked, then, but I don't remember about what.

After class I see Sam walking down Sixth Avenue but I'm not sure it's him so I stop, look around casually, and as he keeps walking I notice he glances back every now and then, looking at me, so I start walking down Sixth Avenue quickly. My shoes crunch over the slushy remains of snow and ice and I walk faster, staring at Sam's back as he approaches a traffic signal. The autumn light is in my eyes and I have to squint.

❧

Something beneath me is grinding horribly and I'm awake and I reach down fast and grab the thing, my cellphone, from beneath my bed, and I sort of moan before opening my eyes and answering the phone because it's mom. "Hi Tad," mom says, and then, "good morning." "Morning, mom," I groan. No one says anything after that so I say, "What do you want?" She says, "I just wanted to make sure you were up for class." My heart is pounding. No one says anything again until mom asks, "Are you coming home this weekend?" I don't say anything and then I say, "No...probably not." She doesn't say anything and I can hear her breathing and then she says, "I miss you." "How's dad?" I ask. My heart is racing now and I can feel my pulse pounding in my forehead. After not saying anything mom says, "I miss you," again. "Okay" is what I say back, and then, "bye." There's static at the other end of the line and then I think mom sighs before saying "Bye, Tad," and I hang up the phone before she can say anything else.

I'm sitting up in bed now, I am amazingly lucid, scanning the room frantically and feeling minor relief when I see that my roommate has already left for class. Time on my phone says 9:10. I jump the three feet to the floor and grab some clean jeans from a drawer beneath my bed. I put the jeans on, still wearing the boxers I slept in, and the jeans slouch on my hips, beginning to slide down to my knees. With an incredible burst of energy I snatch up the burnt jeans from the floor, tear the belt from around the waist, the charred smell of soot and ashes momentarily filling the air, and string the belt across the skinny faded blue jeans I am now wearing, all within a matter of moments. I step out into the kitchen to see Steve sitting at the table, hunched over a bowl of Frosted Flakes, and he nods at me and I say, "hey man," and he says, "yo brah," and I get into the bathroom before anything else can happen. My head is spinning, adrenaline coursing through me, and when I look in the mirror my eyes are red and puffy and my face is gaunt, but this is nothing unusual (the lighting in here fucking sucks) so I pull my toothbrush from its place in the plastic stand on the skinny metal ledge that runs the length of the bathroom wall, slather it with Colgate toothpaste, and begin to brush my teeth violently. Once I feel like I'm going to gag I spit into the sink, rinse off the bristles of my toothbrush, place it back in the four pronged plastic canister that also holds each of my livingmates' toothbrushes, cup my hands under cold running water and slurp that water into my mouth, rinsing and then gargling with ferocity. I spit into the sink and turn instinctively to the shower, but remembering what time it is I say "fuck" and leave the bathroom. Steve is still sitting at the kitchen table and I take a deep breath before I walk to the sink, take a bowl from the cabinet above the sink, look at Steve leering into his bowl and decide not to ask him if I can have some of his Frosted Flakes, grab Brian's box of Wheatabix from atop the refrigerator, set the bowl down on the table (adjacent to, not across from, Steve), open the refrigerator and remove a plastic jug of skim milk, set the jug on the table next to the bowl, sit down at the table, pour some Wheatabix into the bowl, pour milk in, avoid eye contact with Steve which is easy because he's avoiding eye contact with me, remember I don't have a spoon and say "fuck" which makes Steve grunt, stand up, walk to the sink, open the cabinet above it and remove a metal spoon with a plastic blue handle, sit back down at the table, and begin shoveling the Wheatabix into my mouth, not tasting it, just getting it down, getting food into my stomach, as fast as I can. As I continue slurping the milky, wheaty substance I can't help glancing at Steve, and Steve's eyes flick in a different direction, and I immediately look back at my bowl and start tapping my foot. I'm done eating and I bring the bowl to the sink and rinse the bowl out fast and I leave the bowl in the sink when I turn to look at Steve's back, which is still hunched over and I observe the spoon entering and leaving his mouth hypnotically before shaking myself to life and practically dashing into my bedroom. I pick up a large plastic American Apparel bag filled with books because I lost my backpack while shopping at Trash with Sam and I leave my bedroom and before I open the front door I say, "bye," looking in Steve's general direction, and when Steve looks up my eyes focus on him and he nods and then I leave the room and close the door behind me.

In the hallway I look at the floor so I don't look at the door across from me and I keep looking at the floor as I walk rapidly to the elevator. I press the down button on the elevator and take my cellphone from my pocket to check the time – 9:25. Shit. I'm stomping on the ground over and over again and then the elevator gets here and the doors open and two girls and a guy are already in it and they glare at me as I walk into the elevator and I avert my eyes, looking at the elevator panel to see that the button for the lobby is already pressed, so I don't press anything, instead waiting for the doors to close, and I ride the elevator down with three other people I recognize but don't think I've ever met, holding my breath, and when the elevator doors open again it's the lobby and I start breathing hard, walking across the lobby floor before pushing the doors to outside open and taking a cigarette from the pack in my pocket and lighting it. I inhale, then walk down the short flight of steps to the sidewalk and turn right and walk as fast as I can without jogging. I have six blocks to go.

9.

That morning Roger wakes up in the gutter when he sees the people with giant fly heads. At first Roger thinks he's still hallucinating, so he punches himself in the face, and it hurts, and he's still seeing it. The gutter Roger is lying in is in the financial district, so he's mainly watching businessmen and women in suits, carrying backpacks or briefcases, only instead of eyes they all have two huge domes on the sides of their faces. Roger stands up and feels that the ass and legs of his khakis are soaked through, clinging to skin. A fly man brushes past Roger and the feelers where his mouth should be vibrate. Roger feels like he's going to vomit, so he does, on the side of the road. The fly people quicken their pace, walking around him fast, not wanting to make physical contact, the fear that this drunk might become violent pulsing faintly in the back of their heads. Roger looks up and down the street, and, yes, there they all are, people with fly heads, some wearing suits, some wearing jeans, some wearing hoodies, some wearing khakis, but all of them with those bruise-colored domes, those flat silver-blue plates, those twin mouth feelers. Roger staggers out of the gutter, onto the sidewalk, and the fly people walk past him, some of them brushing against him, all of them walking just a little faster when they see him standing there. Roger goes into the nearest subway entrance to sit against a wall and hope this new species will throw him some change.

10.

I'm on Sixth between Sixth and Fifth and moving fast. I'm being propelled forward by the momentum of the cigarette in my hand. Walk five steps, see a person approaching, look away, exhale smoke. Repeat. There is no rhythm to my movement; I am simply rushing along as fast as possible, my heart pounding, trying frantically to get out of here and get to there. This is not as easy as it sounds, because there are now crowds of people walking with and against me, and with every one of them I need to avoid eye contact and, only sightly less important, physical contact. The key to survival is to project absolute disinterest. They aren't human, I tell myself, they're just obstacles, but for some reason this makes it harder. I keep walking.

The cigarette is a precarious thing because I have to time it so that when I breathe out I am not facing anybody in particular so nobody thinks I am blowing smoke at them. It's also precarious because I keep catching my breath and twitching slightly, making it hard to breathe in and out steadily. The good news, though, is that the rising panic just makes me walk faster.

I'm at the corner of Sixth and Fifth and there's traffic. I can't believe it has taken me this long to get here and I know that I will never get to Sixth and Third in time. This knowledge feeds the panic but it also sends a rush of adrenaline through me, the only pleasurable part of walking to class. When the traffic clears I cross the street fast, dodging men and women whose faces make me wince when I accidentally look at them. I continue walking down Sixth and I can see University at the end of the sidewalk when I look long enough. I resolve to look up, above the heads of everyone, and focus on the distance. My legs are carrying me and I don't have to tell them anything. It's my face that worries me. I glance down every now and then; I can't help it; when I do, I sometimes see a blond girl or a man in pea coat and if they look old and oblivious I can look away calmly but if they look young and alert, my age, and most of all hip, I jerk my head fast and hard. The cigarette smoke is starting to make my throat feel dry. I'm at the corner of Sixth and University and I cross.

When I get to Sixth and Broadway a taxi blares its horn and I jump. I try to remember if I've gotten high yet today and when I realize I haven't I attribute this to my tenseness. Try to stay calm I tell myself, try to stay focused, but it's no use. All I can do is keep walking. Pass the Broadway Diner, pass the place that sells cheap and revolting falafel, pass the Mexican place I ate in a few times, pass the buzz and hum and glare of all the human bodies and it's almost too much to take so I raise my cigarette to my lips and suck in hard, barely getting smoke into my lungs, breathing the smoke out of my mouth, and I raise the cigarette again and suck in again and that's the routine that carries me, the instinctive mechanical pulse that's just as involuntary as the slap of my sneakers on the ground, again and again.

At Sixth and Fourth I get across the street fast, cars start moving before I'm even out of the crosswalk, and now there are no more shops and I'm walking past brownstones, an expensive place to live, and there's an old woman walking a dog coming toward me and an Asian guy with a backpack and all of a sudden my throat is so dry I can't breathe in my mouth any more and I try to swallow but I gag, just as I knew I would. I look at the sidewalk, embarrassed, but I feel okay now and I know I won't gag again because this is how it always happens, so I inhale on the cigarette again, more gingerly this time, and I wish I had a bottle of SmartWater.

At the corner of Sixth and Fourth I can see the monolithic Four Brothers inset from the sidewalk, and my cigarette is burned almost down to the filter at this point but I keep smoking it and cross the street. I'm on Sixth and Third and walking past brownstones and small apartments and when I get to Four Brothers there are people loitering outside, none of whom I look at look enough to know if I recognize, and I throw the remains of my cigarette into the street between two parked cars and walk through the revolving door of the gigantic steel building. I look at the security guard, black and dressed like a cop, hand on my wallet in case he asks to see my ID, but he's looking at something else so I walk past him and take my cellphone out of my pocket, and as I'm walking through the lobby to the two huge elevators there's only a smattering of people standing around waiting for their arrival and this not a good sign and I check the time on my cellphone and it's 9:50. A wave of nausea tears through my gut as I realize I'm twenty minutes late for class, but the wave is also comprised of tiny electrons, and those electrons are composed of adrenaline and giddiness, and somewhere I'm thinking, *Who the fuck cares? What difference does it make?*

One of the elevators gets here and I step inside with

four or five other people, some girls in leather skirts and thick glasses and a guy with long hair wearing what looks like a robe who I check out before looking away hastily and pressing the button for the seventh floor. There elevator stops twice before getting to the seventh floor and everyone leaves except an old guy who I now notice, standing in a corner, and his face looks soft and the skin loose and he has thinning white hair and he's wearing big steel-framed glasses and he looks content before he looks at me and I look away.

On the seventh floor I step out quickly and I really want to go to the bathroom because I'm so out of breath I'm almost panting but it's too late for that so I walk down the hall to the right and drink from the water fountain quickly, wishing I had brought a water bottle, and then I turn left and walk to the end of the hall and into class.

I close the door quickly behind me and walk to my regular seat at the front of the room without slowing my pace, looking at the floor, not looking at anything, and when I sit down the first thing I do is look to my left, where Sam is sitting in the desk next to me, and he brushes his hair behind an ear before smiling and whispering, "hey." I smile back at him and whisper, "hey, what's up," and I look at my desk and my heart is more than just fluttering. Sam says, "you're late," in a gentle voice, and I glance up at the whiteboard and Rosemary, our teacher, is gesturing frantically and speaking fast and she doesn't acknowledge that I've just walked in the room, which I am grateful for, and on the board she's written some phrases in black marker that are incomprehensible to me and she's wearing a small, loose white shirt with frilly, almost not-there sleeves, and I'm staring at the space just beneath her shoulder, her thin, tan arm, but then her green eyes stare right at me and I look at Sam, and I giggle and mutter "yeah, I know." Sam

43

makes a flirtatious "tisk-tisk" noise and smiles at me and his blue eyes lock on mine and I can't help but giggle, for real this time. I realize that I haven't taken my backpack off and this kind of embarrasses me so I take my backpack off and place it next to my seat and I lean over and open it and then pretend to look for something in it, rustling around aimlessly for what seems like minutes, before realizing I should take out my notebook so I do and I also take a pen from the bottom of my bag and then I place them on my desk, one on top of the other. I stare at the whiteboard but there's a glare and I still can't read what's been written and the florescent light seems very bright in here and all of a sudden I realize that I'm perspiring intensely so I begin to wipe sweat off my forehead, drying my hand on my jeans. I'm taking deep breaths and trying to slow my heart beat and I'm trying to focus on the closed notebook in front of me but I feel like I can't control my head from twitching this way or that, seeing all the people around me, and then I'm shaking a little bit and I turn to look at Sam who's staring at Rosemary but he winces slightly when he sees peripherally that I'm looking at him and I bite down hard on my lip. I'm hunched over in my seat, tapping my feet on the floor, and I pick up my pen and begin to chew on it as I keep my eyes trained on the notebook's plastic orange cover and I let the teacher's words rush over me, catching only occasional fragments of meaning. At some point Sam turns to me and whispers, "I'm so tired, I didn't sleep last night." I look at him, golden bangs curving towards his pale blue eyes, and it feels like a weight has been lifted from me and I mumble, more enthusiastically now, "Really?" Speaking quietly, Sam says, "Yeah. Well, actually I got two hours of sleep in the study room. I was up almost the whole night working on a lab project." "Really," I ask, with what I hope sounds like enthusiasm, "when's it due?" "Tomorrow," Sam says, looking at my notebook with concern, and I say, "Oh, shit, that sucks," sympathetically, and Sam bristles his nose before saying "Yeah, it does suck. Thanks for saying that." I look away from Sam just as Rosemary spits out, "Sam and Tad stop talking," fast and sharp, hardly breaking her repartee, which I've just now started paying attention to, as I stare at my desk, highly relieved. I pick up my pen and start chewing on it again. Rosemary says something about Thoreau.

11.

Rebecca is working out at Crunch and, she can't believe it, but some piece of shit is eating donuts in front of the window. Right there, behind the giant windows in front of the treadmills, is this skinny kid in a peacoat and thick, black glasses munching on a Dunkin' Donuts. It looks like a frosted cruller, this donut he's holding in one hand, and in the other hand he's holding a giant box of Dunkin' Donuts. This kid, he's grinning as he chews, letting her see every bite, but really she can just see mashed up food moving around and around in his mouth. She's wearing ass-shorts and a tiny pink t-shirt. She feels like she's going to be sick. This kid keeps chewing, grinning now, shoveling the cruller into his mouth. She looks across the street at a Subway and keeps running.

12.

After class Sam and I are standing outside the school smoking cigarettes. We're leaning against the black metal rail with spikes on top that surrounds the overgrowth, finally beginning to die again, on either side of the school's entrance. I smoked a joint down the block a few minutes ago while I was waiting for Sam to come out, because he always leaves class after I do. I'm looking at the faces of the kids exiting the revolving door, walking past us, with detached condescension, and I look at Sam's face, blowing smoke past it, and I ask, "so what are you doing this weekend man?" Sam looks at me, wrinkles his nose, rolls his eyes up in their sockets, and, thinking, says, "um." Sam's skin looks porcelain in the autumn light and his long blond hair is gently brushing against his lips. Sam stops rolling his eyes and looks straight at me, wide-eyed, and the blue of his irises almost makes me look away but I don't and I smile and Sam says, "I have two drawings to work on for Studio Art, so I'll probably do that all Friday, because I only have class till twelve, and then I might go out for a drink with this guy in the army, he asked me to, at Blue Moon I think, but I don't know it might be kind of weird...and then," Sam pauses, "I don't know for the rest of the weekend. I'll probably do homework. I have so much work right now. Did I tell you I didn't sleep last night?" I quickly tell Sam, yes, he did, and he continues, "Yeah, that was really bad. I'm so tired right now. After that class I'm always so tired." I nod vigorously and tell Sam I agree; that class makes me tired too. Sam says, "Yeah. Actually I might start on that essay she just gave us. What do you think you're gonna do for that?" "I dunno, uh," I begin to tell Sam, and then he excitedly tells me, "Yeah, it's really confusing right? Like, what are you supposed to say? It's a really weird topic." I tell Sam that, yeah, it is really weird. "Anyway," Sam says, and smiles, "what are you doing?" Wind blows through the branches of a tree in front of us, its leaves shaking, and I breathe smoke at this image and then look at the girl with the messenger bag and the hoop earrings who is walking past us and then I turn to face Sam, looking at the ground, breathing quickly in and out on my cigarette, and I tell him, "I was thinking of going to the Knitting Factory actually." Sam says "Really?" so brightly that I look at his face and smile. "I don't know who's playing, but I was there last Friday to see this band The Dead Science and it was really cool. It was really fun." Sam is grinning now and he says, "Oh man, that's awesome. I'd *love* to go to the Knitting Factory." All of a sudden Sam looks offended and says, "Why didn't you ask me to go with you on Friday?" "I tried calling you but you didn't pick up!" I yelp. Sam giggles and says, "Oh, really? Oh yeah, I must have been working. Anyway, can I like, come with you? When are you going?" I say, "On Saturday." Sam says, "What time? I have a lot of work to do but," and then he says quickly, "forget it, forget it, it doesn't matter. I can go one night without doing work." I'm grinning and I tell Sam, "Yeah definitely, okay, cool, that's awesome." Sam asks, "So what time on Saturday." I tell him, "Uh, doors at eight, I think." Sam repeats to himself, "doors at eight...okay," and then, smiling, he looks at me and says, "Cool. This is going to be so much fun. I haven't been to the Knitting Factory since last year." "Really?" I ask, trying to stay cool, and Sam says "Yeah! Isn't that weird? Well not weird but like...I should go out more you know? I mean I'm living in the city." I tell Sam I agree with him. My cigarette is almost out and I throw it on the sidewalk before taking out another. "You're a little chain smoker," Sam says cutely, eying me putting the cigarette in my mouth. I giggle and say, "Yeah, I guess so." Sam takes out his cellphone as I'm lighting the cigarette and he says, "Well, I should get going. I have to go to U-Tek to get art supplies and then I have an assload of work." I ask Sam, "Really? When's it due?" Sam says, "Uh, two of the drawings are due tomorrow actually. So I should really get *to* that." I nod and tell Sam, "Yeah, definitely. Do you, uh, wanna smoke another cigarette?" Sam smiles coyly and pulls away from me slightly and half-whines, "no, I should *go*..." and then brightly, "you can walk with me to U-Tek though!" I smile and shake my head no, trying to formulate my words so I don't stammer, and tell him, "no, sorry, I think I'm gonna go back to my dorm...I'm pretty tired." Sam smiles and says frankly, "Yeah, I know, I'm so tired!" Then Sam says, "Okay, well, I'll see you later. I'll see you on Friday!" I smile and kind of blush and I tell Sam, "Okay, see you later," as he says, "bye," and as he begins to turn to walk away he smiles at me and lifts a dainty hand and waves his fingers seductively and his eyes go wide and I smile for real, I can't stop myself, and then I look at the sidewalk and I keep smiling as I inhale on my cigarette, look at the sky, breathe out, and turn to walk away, glancing at the faces of the people around me as I lower my eyes and my lingering smile becomes a smirk and I take it all in.

13.

Tim finishes jerking off and gobs of semen are left dangling from his knotty pubic hair. These days he can't spurt far enough to hit his stomach, so his cum is left clinging to strands of pubes, hanging and then dripping onto his pelvis like melty, milky stalactites. It sort of pisses Tim off, in a frustrated, unconscious way, that his load rarely reaches his chest or even his stomach. His misses the visceral satisfaction he gets from a hot wad ejected with perfect pump-action, mechanical force landing all over his flesh. It's like an orgasm isn't complete without it; there's no real confirmation that anything has happened, no dried crust he can feel if he rubs his torso under his shirt at some point in the day. These days it's like Tim's prick just leaks when he comes, not quite down his shaft but certainly not far enough to mean anything.

Why is this? He doesn't know, but he suspects it has something to do with having to keep quiet now, having to jerk off slower and more deliberately. At home in his attic or basement he could go nuts but living among the others, doors opening and closing all the time, and how fucking *thin* these walls are...it really brings out the paranoia in a sexual being.

Right now there's a mess of toilet paper all over Tim's pubes. That's another pleasure, although much more mild: letting cum dry with a wad of...toilet paper, tissues, whatever's around. Tim's semen is drying right now as he flips open his laptop and goes to Facebook.

14.

On the way back from class a homeless guy stops me at a Walgreens on the corner of Sixth and Fourth. "Excuse me, my man, can you spare a cigarette," he asks, and I tell him, "yeah man," and fumble through my jeans pockets trying to find my pack. "'Preciate it," the homeless guy says, and he's looking into the distance, his eyes darting wildly. I find the pack of cigarettes in the right back pocket of my jeans and I open it, taking one out, and the homeless guy is looking at my hands and licking his lips while I do this. I look into the homeless guy's eyes, which are red and bloodshot, and, extending the hand with the cigarette in it, I automatically assume he's stoned. Course, cold, black fingers brush against mine in the instant the homeless guy takes the cigarette from me, and then he puts it in his mouth, his lips puffy, his face gaunt and hairless, his skin not as dark as most of the black people roaming the streets around here, and he asks me, "Got a light?" I tell him, "oh yeah, totally," and I take a small orange lighter from the same pocket my cigarettes were in and hand it to him. He takes the lighter from me roughly and he flicks the metal wheel with his thumb like it's nobody's business, like this thing better light on the first try and how *dare* it not, and it does, and while he's doing this I throw the remains of my current cigarette on the ground and put a new one between my lips, shoving the pack of cigarettes back in my back pocket just as the homeless guy is holding the lighter out to me and I take it and thank him and he doesn't say anything so I light my cigarette, put the lighter in my pocket, and turn to walk away just as the homeless guy stops me by saying, "You go to school around here?" I turn back to the homeless guy and nod, telling him, "yeah man, I do." "What school," the homeless guy says, as he squints and blows smoke past my face. I'm looking at another homeless guy sitting in the marble vestibule outside Walgreens and there's a wool blanket covering his lower body and it doesn't look like he has any legs as I say, "uh, Four Brothers." The homeless guy chuckles and says, "Four Brothers! Jesus," and I'm not sure what he means and a well-dressed white woman is now bending over the homeless guy on the ground, who is leaning against a marble pillar, staring straight ahead at the revolving door of the Walgreens, and I notice a McDonalds cup at where his feet might be and a cardboard sign with something written on it leaning against his chest, and the woman is saying something about a sandwich and I suddenly want to get out of here very badly so I look in the face of the homeless guy I gave the cigarette to and say, "Yeah. I need to go, man." "You got five bucks," the homeless guy says, looking straight at me now, and he's not squinting anymore and I look down and say, "no, sorry." "Come on man," the homeless guy says, "you have enough money to buy cigarettes. I know you must have *at least* five bucks." I look into the homeless black guy's red eyes and say, "I don't have any money with me, man. I'm short on cash." "How 'bout we go to an ATM then," the homeless guy says, and I say, "No thanks, dude. I need to go." I turn and start walking away from the Walgreens and I hear the homeless guy make a *pfft* sound and then say, "Aight, have fun in school, college boy," from behind me. I'm walking across Fourth and taking fast, short drags off my cigarette and fortunately I'm almost away from the homeless guy. I try to think if I need to pick up weed and I think I have enough left for at least tonight and I keep walking.

15.

Tim is lying on his back and studying the thick blue vein that runs from the base of his cock up to the middle of his shaft before stopping and splitting into two thinner veins that run horizontally and wondering how this would look to an outside observer when he hears the handle on his bedroom door turning. Shit. Tim pulls up his pants quickly, grabs his laptop from the floor, opens the screen and goes to Facebook before looking over to see who just walked in, and, fortunately, it's just Tad, alone. Tim is relieved because Tad is perpetually out of it and even if he suspected, on some level, that Tim was fondling his cock, it just wouldn't register on the surface. Tim is browsing Facebook with mild interest now, accepting friend requests from four people and checking out pictures to see if he knows any of them. Tad is saying something but it's remote, like white noise. Partially that's because Tad's voice sounds kind of like white noise, a weird, grating tone that's somehow high-pitched and low, stuttering, and gargley at the same time, and partially it's because Tad is always stammering about something that hardly makes sense or matters. Tim is still clicking through

Facebook when words finally register through the din, Tad saying, "Dude," over and over again. Tim turns from the laptop screen and looks at Tad, who looks at the ground and says something. Tim turns back to the laptop and starts looking at some pictures of himself when he realizes that he missed what Tad said and Tad is still talking. Tim says, "What?," and then looks down at his jeans. He realizes that he left his fly open. Shit. He pulls the zipper up.

16.

I'm stoned. My name is Tad. I sigh and look over at my roommate, who's sitting on his bed, also stoned. The lights are on and the movie we're watching is *Dan in Real Life*. The movie is really weird, almost to the point of being upsetting, so I'm not really paying attention to it. I'm lying on my bed, legs folded Indian style, and I keep looking at my fingers, which are long and thin and one of my favorite parts of my body, and then looking across the room at my roommate, mulling over the question in my head before eventually deciding to ask it: "Hey man, do you want to order cookies?"

My roommate looks up from his laptop and stares across the room at me. I look back at my fingers, begin sucking my right thumb, and then look back at my roommate. He's not saying anything and still staring at me. I'm getting nervous and I ask him, "uh, do you?" My roommate still says nothing and then he says, "that's what I was just doing," before grinning. I grin back and say, "shit man, I totally forgot." My roommate grins wider and, almost laughing, says, "did you really?" I say, "yeah dude, I totally did," and for some reason I'm not grinning any more. My roommate says, "wow," his face going blank, and then he looks back at his laptop. I lean back into my bed, looking back at my fingers, feeling slightly embarrassed, trying to remember what kind of cookies I asked for and not wanting to ask my roommate to remind me.

This is when someone starts pounding on the door and I jump, startled. My eyes are darting around the room when the voice says, "Hey. It's Brian." I fix my eyes on my roommate now, awaiting instruction, and he looks from the door into my eyes and says, "Let him in I guess." I crawl to the end of my bed and open the door from there. Brian walks into the room and, shutting the door behind him before standing in place and staring out the window, says, "It fucking reeks out there," and then, looking over at me, "can I have some?" I tell Brian, "sure dude," but I can feel myself starting to panic because of what Brian just said about the kitchen smelling like grass, and, who knows, maybe the hallway too, so without thinking I ask Brian, "does it smell in the hallway?" Brian has been standing over my desk, looking at things on it, and without looking up he says to me, "I don't know, I haven't been out there," and scoffs, and I feel a pang of remorse about having asked that question. The remorse is almost immediately swept away by the rising panic and I look across the room at my roommate and ask, "dude should we spray something," and when he doesn't respond or look away from his laptop screen I ask, "Tim, do you think we should spray something?" Tim looks at me and says, "Yeah, I guess so...if it smells out there then yeah." I quickly get down off my bed and walk to my desk, which Brian is still standing over, and when I'm standing beside him he glances up at me and asks, "where...is the weed?" I grab a can of lemon Lysol off the top shelf of my desk and tell Brian, "I think it's on Tim's desk." I look over there and see that it is, and then I look at my roommate, and my roommate is glaring at Brian as Brian walks to my roommate's desk, and I'm pretty sure Brian notices and I walk out of the room, into the kitchen, where I can't tell if it smells like grass but I shut the bedroom door behind me, watching the white tiled kitchen floor, which looks bright in the glare of the fluorescent light, and then I start spraying the Lysol into the air, turning in circles to spray wildly. I stop when it smells noticeably like lemon in here, and then I walk to the front door and spray its edges, the gaps between door and door frame, trying to get the scent of lemon into the hallway. I put the can down and walk back into my bedroom, bracing myself for what might be happening between Brian and Tim.

Inside Brian is taking a hit off the piece, standing by the window, and Tim is sitting at the end of his bed and telling him, "dude...I think you're doing it wrong." Brian coughs and looks at the piece in his hand before asking, "Is this clogged or something?" Tim sighs and says, "no, you just don't know how to hit it correctly." Brian looks up, exasperated, and says, "well, what am I supposed to do? I mean..." Tim gets off his bed, his body touching Brian's, and he sighs again before saying, "Here. I'll hold the carb for you and I'll light it. All you need to do is breathe in." Tim is audibly annoyed and Brian does what he says as Tim holds the lighter to the bowl, one finger over the carb. I watch this happening before sitting on my bed and trying to watch the movie, but that's too hard to do so I go back to watching Tim and Brian. Tim has released his finger from the carb and I can hear Brian breathing in and then seconds later coughing hard, smoke surrounding him. "There," Tim says, "You got a hit." Brian looks at the smoking piece in his hand and says, "I don't know. I don't really feel like I did. It feels harsh for some reason. Are you sure it isn't clogged?" Tim sighs and says, "No, Brian, it isn't clogged. Watch, I'll do it." Tim takes the piece and the lighter from Brian's hands and lights the bowl expertly, inhaling and then exhaling smoke out the window. He doesn't cough. Tim says, "See?" Light from the building across the street is glinting off Brian's white glasses and Brian looks confused, maybe even dejected, and he says, "well, whatever." Tim places the piece and the lighter on his desk and then Brian picks the piece up, studies it, and puts it down. Brian asks, "What are you guys watching?" Tim tells him, "*Dan in Real Life*," and then they both look at me and I look down at my fingers. "Oh nice," Brian says. "I love that movie. Do you guys mind if I watch it with you?" Tim is now sitting back on his bed, doing stuff on his laptop, and without looking up he mumbles, monotone, "Yeah I guess so." Tim then looks at me with what I think is a glare and I look at him with wide eyes and an expression I can't define, and then Brian turns to me and asks, "Mind if I borrow your chair?" I look at Brian and say, maybe over-eagerly, "Yeah dude, totally." Brian drags the chair from my desk to the back of the room where he sits in it before staring at the TV. I'm looking at my fingers and I ask, "When are the cookies coming?" before putting my thumb back in my mouth and sucking.

17.

"**F**irebomb the elevator...I like where this is going," the Vampire said, which seemed like a strange idea, coming from him of all people. "Knock it off, we don't have time for that shit," I tell him, and his eyes seem to droop a little and his fangs stick out over his top lip. I sigh, realizing that he's upset, and look at my watch and think "just two more hours of this shit."

When we step off the elevator into the lobby of my apartment the Vampire's eyes bulge and turn red and I'm hoping the guard won't notice but wondering what would happen if he did, but me and the Vampire get by without incident. Walking past the guard the Vampire stares straight ahead and stands up tall and walks swiftly, my kinda guy. But then, when we're outside and it's time to hail a cab, the Vampire apparently realizes that this facade of normalcy is too much for him, and he puts his hood up over half his face. I laugh at this gesture and the Vampire scowls at me. Hey, whatever. The guy is probably just off his gourd waiting for this next stop. Who could blame him?

Outside Veronica's studio apartment in the east village

I pound the door fast and hard, the Vampire totally fucking freaking out at this point--he's abandoned the idea of concealment entirely, his hood torn from his cape, and his veins are popping underneath pale, white skin, and when he's not shrieking animalistically he's shouting things like "Napalm the church!" and "Semtex the subway!" and "Nuke the East Coast!" and his fangs are long and sharp and glistening. I feel like I should be doing something about this, but honestly, what the fuck can I do?, so I just get the Vampire to Veronica's place as fast as possible, telling the cab driver to hurry the fuck up, that my friend is sick, and the cab driver looking utterly unfazed in the rearview mirror.

I can hear Veronica approaching the front door and I shout "Come on Veronica!...Do you hear this shit?!" Veronica snaps the door open in a rush and she gasps when she sees the Vampire and he's shrieking wildly, his fangs pointed up towards the sun, and it pisses me off that I have to tell Veronica "He just needs the shit." She nods, blinking, and hurries inside to get it and the Vampire and I follow her in and I slam the door fast, causing Veronica to jump and turn around and shout "You can't fucking bring him in here!" to which I respond "You want me to fucking leave him outside? Just get the shit and he'll be fine!", and Veronica does so. I'm melting the heroin on a spoon and Veronica's holding the syringe and standing very still and watching the Vampire do his freak out bit and then it's done melting and Veronica sucks it up and hands me the syringe and I approach the Vampire, my heart pounding, but when he sees what I have he stops freaking out and he, too, stands very still and allows me to inject it into a vein on his forearm, massive and pulsing and impossibly alive. Thirty seconds later I leave with the Vampire.

Everything should be fine now that the Vampire's got his fix, and that was the first and only stop we had to make before the airport. On the ride out to JFK the Vampire sits passively in the backseat next to me and the cab driver gives us only casual, routine, glances of disapproval and when we get there, as if on cue, as if this has all been planned, my cellphone rings. It's my CIA contact, the usual guy, and I answer the phone instinctively, "Yeah, we're here." "Good. I'm on my way," he says, and then clicks off. Me and the Vampire are standing in customs, his fangs gone, his eyes glazed and only half-visible beneath gray eyelids, and it takes about three minutes for the CIA guy to get to me. The CIA guy looks the Vampire over once, casually, before giving me a brusque "Good work," and then a "The transfer will go through in ninety seconds," and I'm happy because that means I just got paid but I can't help looking over my shoulder at them, the CIA guy leading the Vampire forward, the Vampire not resisting, and I hear the CIA guy tell him "Good boy...you'll be put to good use," and I kind of shudder and when I turn back around they're walking down a narrow hallway, a large wooden box at the end, and then I turn around a final time and try to hail a cab.

The election is tomorrow.

18.

Beat us up for fun and profit, Walter said to the strangers, but they couldn't hear him because the slot machines were making noise for a Winner. Samantha looked like she was on cocaine, her eyes darting from the blare of the pay-off to the face of Bill, her boyfriend, and the trembling in her fingertips suggested the suppression of something violent. The strangers looked at each other before moving closer to us, blocking out the sun. When the one on the left stepped out of the smoke and told Sam she better get out of here, quick, and jabbed a sweaty finger at her face, Walter spit the Vodka he was drinking across the casino's tiled carpet and told the man "hey, come on, we just want to hurt." Overhead a ceiling fan stirred smoke. A cigarette butt was dropped, and then the stranger in the cowboy hat punched Walter in the throat, who staggered backwards coughing blood.

Walter collapsed on his back, his eyes bulging, blood gurgling through his lips and then launched upward as he coughed—low and unrepentant, the cough of smokers, and then he never coughed again. Overhead a ceiling fan stopped, and then the buzz of electricity was flowing freely through the place. I scrambled backwards and grabbed for Sam's hand but she was staring at Bill, intent, so I turned around and ran. The puke-green of the carpet was my only thought even as the bouncers started to descend, because they rushed past me, oblivious to my presence even though I was running full-speed, panting uncontrollably, in the opposite direction. I later learned the reason Sam had been staring at Bill was because the malignant tumor that had been prominently growing on his forehead the past six months had utterly ruptured, leaking blood and pus down his face and into his eyes. Bill's irises were very large in the photos I saw. At the exit was where I turned around in time to see Sam's skull explode into disc and tissue, her body collapse sideways across Bill's, and also where I lost consciousness.

A neon blur of orange and green rings through me and I'm sitting in an all-night diner trembling over a cup of coffee and I'm clamping my fingers across my mouth to suppress dry heaves and then I'm in the bathroom vomiting once, twice, three times and I drop to my knees hard but the pain ringing in my kneecaps seems distant and I'm leaning my head against the toilet seat and thinking about Sam and then laughing, grunting and nothing matters and then I'm outside and amazed to see my car here so I rush inside and hastily do four lines of the coke locked in the glove box that I promised myself I'd never do. Back inside the diner I'm feeling better, taking deep breaths, hoping no one's looking at me but then realizing who gives a shit, and I take a sip of the coffee and feel good. A fly buzzes behind my ear and the fluorescent lighting in this place makes it seem like something without time. This is where I felt my cellphone vibrate in my pocket, feeling tingly against my thigh, and opened it to read the text message from Julia that said "hey did you register to vote?"

19.

There is a dead man in the driveway, and Tom still has time to kill. He paces the driveway, becomes overwhelmed by his heartbeat, tries to take deep breaths from his abdomen, like Max told him to do, to slow down, or maybe it was to speed up, and Tom looks at the moon.

Looking at the moon has a tranquilizing effect on Tom. The distance, it makes it so the corporeal world doesn't matter. The luminescence is also very calming, like the expensive natural lighting fixture Tom's parents bought for him after he tried to commit suicide in February. It is November, now, though, and those things don't matter anymore. The first thing that matters is, the man whose brain is splattered all over Tom's parents' driveway is starting to leak blood onto his shoes (small driveway, you see), and the second thing that matters is he isn't high.

Truth be told Tom is, practically, paralyzed with fear, gulping down hard, feeling his heart slam itself into his ribcage and then his shoulder blade, trying to breathe in deep, from the abdomen, but he can't complete a breath without shaking violently. He is only here because the cleaners aren't, but even if they were, he doesn't think he'd be able to move his body without humiliating himself. He breathes in deep, trying not to shake, exhales at the moon, wishing he had a cigarette, and then his head jerks and his eyes focus on the man's head, which is now just a ragged stump with two huge folds of skin hanging down past the neck, and gooey lumps of brain matter circle the ground, fragments of skull with black hair sticking straight up out of intact scalp, and Tom heaves and doubles over, vomiting. A car horn sounds, as if on cue, and the cleaners are here.

They get out of the car. The driver is blond, tall, and muscular; the passenger is brunet, tall, and well-muscled.

"This is repulsive," the blond guy says, grinning, as he makes his way over to where Tom is slouched, lit brightly by lights that line the front steps and flowerbeds of the outside of the two-bedroom Victorian house. Tom is still hunched over, groaning quietly, a large puddle of vomit at his feet. The blond guy looks at the puddle, then at the remains of the dead man's face, laughs, and says, "you did good, kid."

Tom isn't sure what he did but he looks up into the face of the blond guy, trying not to shake, focusing on his breathing, and the face looks genuinely warm so Tom smiles and says, "thanks."

"You should probably idle in the car," the brunet tells Tom, walking over, carrying a leather Gucci suitcase, his cool olive eyes not untempting. "In case if anyone shows up, just tell them we're taking stuff to the dump."

Tom nods, and when the brunet guy smiles and winks at him Tom smiles back and looks away, probably blushing.

The brunet hands Tom the keys to his car, a Toyota, and Tom gets inside and starts the ignition, idling outside his own house as two guys clean a dead man from his driveway. Tom tries to distract himself from the situation by watching the brunet's ass, plump and heart-shaped in his tight jeans, as the brunet lays down a tarp. Tom's getting mildly hard and trying to locate the bulge of a cock in the brunet guy's, or even the blond guy's, jeans when they both take body-length raincoats from the Gucci bag and put them on, obstructing all shapeliness. Then they take shovels from the bag and lift the dead guy's body with the shovels, blood leaking from the stump, making a thick trail on the asphalt as they lift it onto the tarp. Tom looks away, then, and focuses on keeping his hands from shaking by gripping the steering wheel.

Tom sits there breathing in and out, trying to be steady but catching his breath every time he breaths in or out too much. He puts a hand on his abdomen, the way Max told him too, and tries to fill it, penetrating his body with oxygen more fully and relaxing him at the same time. Someone is shouting; opening the car door Tom sees its the blond guy, asking him where the hose is. Rather than directing the blond guy to it Tom gets out of the car and walks over to it, hidden behind some big-leaved bushes at the side of the house. Tom did this, came over here, risked having to see the brunet scrape the last solid bits of skull onto the edge of his shovel and dump them onto the tarp, to lead the blond guy to the hose so he could ask "can I have a cigarette?" He gives Tom one, Tom doesn't thank him because he doesn't think his voice won't tremble, and he doesn't need a light because he has a lighter in his pocket, so he lights the cigarette and quickly walks back to the car. "Hey, uh, don't smoke in my car dude. Roll down the window and stick your head out." Tom nods, opens the car door, rolls down the window before he gets in, careful to hold his arm through the open window as he enters the car.

It's night. 2:32 (am) according to the clock on the dashboard of the blond guy's car. Time doesn't mean much to Tom anymore, but he guesses it never really did because he never wore a watch. Tom sighs, inhales on the cigarette, exhales with his head out the window. He diverts his attention from the activity in his driveway, trying to find the moon but it must be behind him because all he can see are the tips of oak trees. *All this for some H*, Tom thinks, groaning to himself. Why do things have to be so complicated?

The truth was he had just allowed a murder to happen on his private property, so the least they could do was treat him with more respect, give him the junk *now*, not later. But Tom is still a sophomore in high school, which puts him at the lowest potential rung of any adult world dealings. And this is the adult world, Tom knows this very well; all things considered, he's been handling it pretty well. No real signs of addiction; there were cravings, sure, but nothing more extreme than, for example, the need to eat when you are starving, and Tom had learned to tame that impulse years before. Sitting now, smoking, he watches the trees and the dark sky behind them, hearing the faint rustle of wind, seeing an occasional black bird between the leaves or maybe not, and the brunet guy taps on the driver side window, holding the suitcase in one hand, and says "we're finished."

They aren't wearing raincoats anymore and although the driveway is soaked and white soapy water trickles down the street into the gutter there is no sign of red or solid matter of any kind. It looks smooth and clean and flat, the asphalt as meaningless as ever, not a brief resting place for a dead man but a place to park cars in. Tom is relieved, and he finishes the cigarette as he steps out of the car. The brunet puts the suitcase in the trunk, then walks over to Tom.

"Thanks for this, buddy," he says, and his eyes tell Tom he means it. "When you told us your parents were going to Shanghai for a week, well, you know..." There is a pause and then the brunet says, "the timing was *perfect*. There was really no other place we *could* have done it." Tom nods, breathing and moving somewhat normally now even though his daily 4 mg each of lithium and klonopin felt like they wore off hours ago. The brunet leans forward and kisses Tom's cheek. Tom is so flustered he might have gotten a boner if it wasn't for the second most important thing, pushing itself against the frontal lobes of his brain now that the first was out of the picture, and Tom says "so uh I can have the stuff now right?"

The brunet laughs, then quickly stops. His lips are pursed. "Yes, you can have it now," the brunet says. "George?"

The blond guy, who has been sitting the driver seat of his car, seems to know what the brunet guy wants because he reaches over to open the glove compartment and takes out a medium-sized baggy packed with white. The blond guy gets out, hands it to the brunet guy, who says "thanks, bro." Tom wonders if these guys play football, and then what it would be like if they came on his face. The brunet guy hands Tom the baggie of heroin. Tom thanks him. The brunet guy nods, his face blank, and just when it seems he's going to turn away he smiles and then winks, and then he goes.

Tom's holding the bag in his jacket pocket. He's pushing his fingers lightly against its contents. When they first asked Tom if they could use his driveway, he thought about asking who was going to get killed, but he didn't need to because they immediately told him, "we need to kill a guy who owes us money." Tom was so taken by this honesty that he decided right then and there, in the school cafeteria, to let them do it. He knew he'd be getting drugs out of it, so why not? He wondered if these guys played football and assumed they probably did. As Tom watches the car drive away, the murky foam of the cleaning products they used to clean all evidence of human residue from the asphalt, gurgling at the bottom of the driveway, he wonders if he made the right choice. He's finding it difficult to think straight, but he guesses he did. He realizes he doesn't know the brunet guy's name as the Toyota turns a corner. He doesn't think about this very long, instead reminding himself that his parents won't be home for another four days and getting excited all over again, and he goes inside to get high.

It's election day.

20.

We call what we do digital.

Pop is saying this to me and I'm sort of nodding. What he's saying seems to matter. "Really," he says, "we're just the mechanisms of fate. The mechanics, I mean." I sort of grin and tell him "dude, I get what you're saying." We're in a secret bunker miles beneath the Sahara Desert; how many miles, no one truly knows. "One more time," Pop says, and pauses, and the look in his eyes tells me this is gonna take a while, so I interrupt him and ask "do you want to keep shooting?" Pop says, "totally." I put more spank in the air-shaft and let him go first. He doesn't thank me. I don't mind because this is his dad's bunker and he doesn't have to let me be here, and we *definitely* shouldn't be shooting spank in here.

So when he passes me the air-shaft I keep grinning and thank him and shoot two pills hard down my throat, swallow hard before smiling to say "this is good shit. All I can think about, though, is how fucking cool it is to be in a secret bunker, miles beneath the Sahara Desert. "This is going to be big, Kevin," and his eyes go serene, which I kind of like, "and we are here, here at the beginnings of it." My head is racing now and kind of pulsing from the spank and I realize that I need to calm down, but his words are ringing in my ears and I believe them and I keep hearing "the beginnings of it" in my mind and then, for some reason, "we call what we do digital."

I'm awake.

My head hurts a lot.

I am more or less ready for it, though, because I've been shooting spank every day since I met Pop, so I open my eyes.

The pain is unexpectedly sharp and I suddenly feel like I am going to vomit so I turn to wake up Pop, who is sitting up-right on the edge of a table, asleep.

"Pop, man," I groan, and instantly his eyes snap open.

I'm crawling on my hands and knees in an effort to stand up, watching the carpet spin as I stagger across the floor towards Pop, and I shut my eyes hard and gag, slapping my hand to my mouth, and when I swallow and open my eyes Pop is alert on the edge of the table, watching me.

I open the cabinet, find a bottle of water, swallow it down, and immediately burp several times. The cabinet has polished wooden doors. There is a wide array of alcohol within it. I am lucky Pop's dad stocked bottled water.

Pop is still sitting on the edge of that huge metal table in the middle of the room, sitting there watching me, and it looks like he's being lit by a spotlight from above. I look up and realize it's the track lighting on the ceiling. Feeling comforted, I begin to make my way over to Pop, noticing all the empty beer cans and pill canisters sprawled across the metal tabletop, thinking, *god, did we really do that much?*

Then I'm standing over the table and I notice diagrams for what appear to be missiles and instantly Pop swings his legs up over these, sitting up on the table, and he smiles at me and says "Good morning." I look into his hazel eyes, coolly noticing the blonde hair gently splayed across his forehead, his porcelain skin, thinking, *is this for real?* He slides the documents off of the table with his legs and lets them scatter across the floor and I'm wondering what Pop did last night after I passed out but Pop interrupts this train of thought by saying "We should go."

"Can I, like, use a computer first? I need one bad." "Down here?" is his response, as if this should be enough explanation, and maybe it should, but then he says "Remember what we said about objective realities, Kevin" and I realize he's right. We should go.

He nods. He gets down from the table and leads me (by the hand, which makes be blush) to the elevator doors and pushes the up button. As we wait for the elevator to arrive Pop lets go of my hand and, staring at the elevator doors, tells me "The revolution is nearer than you think. We are the new movers and shakers, the arbiters of fate; we decide how the world should be," and he pauses before smiling to say "Let's get you that computer when we get up there." He turns to face me, taking my hand again, and he looks into my eyes and smiles bigger than before, and I smile back. The elevator is here.

We get inside. The red and white of the jumpsuit Pop is wearing fills my eyes pleasingly, but I hastily look away, instead focusing on the tiny room with the floor-to-ceiling cabinet and gigantic metal table towering over it. There are still beer cans and pill bottles all over the the table and floor. "Won't your dad notice those?" I ask him, alarmed. "My dad never comes in this room." The elevator doors close. Pop is holding the button to go up and we're ascending at a fairly rapid pace.

When we get to the surface we step out onto a landing pad, where dense, brown sand is gleaming in all directions around us. Pop makes a little twirling motion with his finger indicating that I should turn around, and I smile because I think this part is cute, and he says "Close your eyes" and then puts the blindfold on me. I can hear Pop radioing for the helicopter and wind is whipping around me and the sound of the wind is soon the only thing I can hear.

The next thing I hear is Pop saying "Oh, I almost forgot." Noise-blocking ear things are placed on my head and I open my mouth to thank him, but for some reason I get sand in my mouth and instead I just spit. Pretty soon the helicopter arrives. I can hear the motor dully and wind continues to rush against me and Pop takes my hand and leads me to the helicopter, helping me find footing on the rail to step up into it. We sit on a cushioned seat. I hear Pop shout something to the pilot and the helicopter takes off and then Pop places a hand on my shoulder and I think I hear him say, "Don't worry, you'll be able to take those off soon."

On the jet ride home, Pop hands me his laptop. He takes it from a backpack in an overhead compartment, and places it in my hands. "Be careful," he says, before he lets me take it from him. "There are some scripts on here that you absolutely *must not run*. You'll know them if you find them." I nod, looking into eyes that appear genuinely frightened, and this unnerves me so much I actually say "yes, I promise."

Pop lets me take the laptop; I place it on the table in front of me. We're sitting on a cushioned barstool/sofa, which juts out from an inside wall of the jet in a wooden frame. The wood is polished and looks really nice. Very expensive. It looks like the wood on the cabinet doors in that room at the bunker, only thicker, obviously.

This is a private jet so when I had discovered the bottles of spank in my backpack that I didn't know I had left there, I didn't panic, but instead went into the bathroom and shot three through an air-shaft hastily. I thought about asking

Pop if he wanted any but decided that if the bottles were in my backpack it was probably my spank, and I wasn't sure if I wanted to share it yet. Pop's laptop is booting up as I'm blinking into the half-circle of spherical lights on the ceiling above us, then looking across the jet and wondering if I can make myself another drink.

The computer makes a pleasing noise as Windows Vista loads onto the screen but I decide to ask Pop if I can have another drink, and when he looks up and tells me "sure" I ask him if he wants one, too, and he says "whatever you're having." I pour us two glasses of Jack Daniel's Single Barrel and return to my seat next to Pop. I hand him a glass and he smiles warmly and says "Thanks." "A toast"?, I suggest, and Pop laughs and says "Sure. To the new age." He grins and drinks the whiskey fast, appearing to savor it for a moment before gulping it down, and I smile and drink mine.

I wonder if we can smoke a joint in here is my next thought, but I quickly dismiss it, remembering Pop doesn't like grass.

I turn to the computer, open up Firefox, check my gmail account and encounter an array of new messages: a school news bulletin, an email from my mom with the subject "What day are you getting back, again"?, a receipt from iTunes, a weekly update from celebrityboobs.com, notifications that new posts have been made in various threads I'm tracking on several forums. I open the email from my mother.

"Hi. I was wondering what day you're getting back from wherever you are. I need to know how much to make for dinner. -Mom." I can't remember my mom ever cooking dinner so the second sentence confuses me, but I ignore it and type "Tomorrow. We're on the plane coming back now." and send it to her.

I look at Pop, who's dialing something frantically into

his cellphone, and I'm feeling mellow from the spank so I decide to hack a website. I open the clock on the lower right of the screen, to time myself. I try to think of a word to type into google and for some reason decide on "pop." The first two results that come up are Wikipedia articles but the third one is a site called "brainpop.com." I click on it. I become giddy at the thought of messing with the flash animations on their html front page, but Pop's computer for some reason does not have PhotoShop, nor "gimpshop," installed, so I check the clock on the windows task bar and settle on changing the page to read WE LOVE COCK ;) with a picture of a severed penis (found via a .02 second search on images.google of the term "erotic") below it. I look down at the clock. Four minutes and nineteen seconds. I smile.

Closing the clock, I elbow Pop, showing him what I've done. He laughs out loud and, tilting his head back and squeezing his eyes shut, says "Oh man. Nicely done," still grinning.

"I'm trying to convince myself that I'm not wasting my time."

"And?" Pop asks.

"Well," I say, stuttering....

"Well, I guess what I'm saying is doing a variety of things is usually worse than doing one thing passionately. Also, fuck the internet, forum interaction should never exist on a greater scale than real-life interaction on a day-to-day basis; the digital world is only there to be exploited mercilessly by whomever has the means to do so. Find something to do, and do it a lot or do it well. This is life we are talking about here. You are 18. Stop struggling to achieve so much; in love, especially."

I recite the mantra with glazed eyes. Suddenly I can't bear the thought of reciting my friend's name ever again.

"Oh, and you cannot smoke pot in here."

I am baffled as to why my friend would say this, at this time, and my only thought, stoned on spank, is that he must be able to read minds. Little did I know this wouldn't be far from the truth.

21.

that's more than bonnie and clyde got

The rest of the week passes fast. The next morning is Tuesday and I don't have class until the afternoon and when I wake up it's not because of my mom calling me, which is a relief. I eat some cereal and take a few hits of grass before walking to 3D. 3D is boring but I'm high and some of the models make me laugh. I have a long term project to make a model that says something about politics in New York and when I get back to the dorms I smoke more grass and play Call of Duty 4 on my computer and watch South Park on Comedy Central. My roommate is there which makes me slightly uncomfortable but it isn't too bad and we go outside to smoke cigarettes together. I guess Obama won because this kid from inside is playing the national anthem on his guitar and people are running down the block shouting and laughing and someone who I guess is my roommate's friend comes up to him and tells him, while I look away, there's a big party at Union Square to celebrate Obama and Paul Dano is there already and a bunch of other celebrities are supposed to show up soon. Cool. The next two days go by similarly, minus the election stuff, plus I have 2D and Studio Art instead of 3D and I smoke grass with my roommate and Amanda and then Kay instead of just my roommate and we watch the movies *Mr. & Mrs. Smith* and *Mean Girls* instead of South Park.

On Friday I don't have class so I spend the day trying to find someone to sell me cocaine, because I know I won't make it through the night with Sam without it. When I wake up at eleven my roommate is still here and I ask him if he knows anyone who might have coke. My roommate says no but if I find any to get him some. I decide to take the elevator down to the fifth floor where someone named Kevin who sold Steve coke at the beginning of the year lives. I knock on Kevin's door and he opens it with a towel wrapped around his lower body, his chest bare, his long red hair brushed back, damp and darting out wildly. I take my eyes from Kevin's sizable pectorals and look at his mouth when I ask him if he has any coke. He says, "Yeah," and he turns around and walks through the kitchen, which juts off into another tiled hallway with one single room and one double room, into the single room and I follow him.

Kevin's bedroom is half the size of mine and my roommate's but he's the only one living in it. He sits down at his desk and I'm looking at the tube of cream and box of tissues on the windowsill next to his bed when he asks me how much I want. I tell him a dub and I hear Kevin opening drawers in his desk while I look around the room at floral patterns on the carpet and Native American designs on the wall. Kevin pushes his chair back from his desk and stands up, facing me, to hand me a small baggie of white powder. I look into Kevin's pale blue eyes and thank him, my heart pounding, and then I look at the ground and take my wallet out and hand him a twenty. Kevin doesn't say anything and he puts the bill in his pocket and I put the coke in mine, and when he continues to stand there, not saying anything, I turn around and walk out of his bedroom and through the kitchen and into the hall.

The show is at eight and I haven't spoken to Sam since yesterday, when I called him and we talked for fifteen minutes about how much he hates his roommate while I agreed heartily with everything he said and then we promised to see each other tomorrow at seven thirty. Right now it's six fifteen according to the clock on my cellphone, and I'm checking my cellphone at regular intervals in case Sam has texted me and I missed it and to read over old texts I've gotten from him, trying to determine different ways they could be interpreted. I'm high and I'm browsing Facebook, looking at photos of people in my classes who haven't friended me, while my roommate, also high, watches dubbed episodes of Naruto on Youtube. The following hour and a half seem to fly by quickly, with Brian entering the room and complaining about not being high for at least twenty minutes, and then Steve barging in and smoking my grass without asking, and by the time it's time to go I'm not even very high anymore so I pack a bowl and smoke it before leaving. I'm at the front door when I remember the coke and I rush into the bathroom, fast, to do two huge lines on the metal sill over the sink and in front of the mirror, but I like them so much I cut two more lines and snort them back hard, savoring the sting and the water in my eyes. Cool.

Outside in the hallway I'm checking my cellphone repeatedly as I walk to the elevator. No word from Sam, which makes me feel somewhat more nervous than I already do even though it shouldn't. The elevator doors open to reveal three stoic faces and when I get in I glance at each quietly loathing face coolly before glancing at the panel of buttons in the elevator, seeing that the button for the lobby is already pressed, and mashing the door-close button before taking a step sideways away from the eyes of the kids I don't recognize but whom I know hate me so that I'm standing directly in front of the closed doors and feeling the elevator plummet and when the elevator doors open I walk across the lobby, keeping my eyes fixed on the floor, and I leave the building holding the door open for one of the kids from the elevator who hates me for reasons I can't understand and he makes a noise that sounds like a half-grunt, half-snicker and I'm walking down the four steps in front of the building and turning right onto Sixth Avenue because I have to get to the dorms between Third and Fourth, where Sam lives, by the school, and I'm checking my cellphone again and still not seeing a message from Sam so I put the cellphone back in my pocket and take out a cigarette, staring at the sidewalk and dodging all forms of moving human life the whole time, and I'm lighting the cigarette just as I'm about to arrive the corner of Sixth and Sixth. I stand at the corner waiting for the light to change, looking from person to person with whiplash speed, until I get so uncomfortable I just look in the direction of the passing cars, waiting for a gap in traffic so I can walk across the street, which I will continue to do at every intersection I reach tonight. Two more taxi cabs past and then I'm walking again, inhaling hard on the cigarette in my hand and holding smoke in my lungs until there's enough of a gap among the people walking my way that I can exhale without getting smoke in their faces.

I'm on Fifth and walking fast past bars and people laughing and talking to each other and I'm snaking my way through them, not daring to look a single one in the eyes, gritting my teeth and clenching my jaw tightly shut except when I feel the need to take a drag off this cigarette, which is probably every ten seconds. I'm feeling the pockets of my jeans, making sure I still have my wallet and my cellphone, even though I have no reason to think I lost them, and I take out my cellphone and open it and see that Sam still hasn't contacted me which is actually kind of a relief as I approach University. There's a Quiznos to my left which I look at, drawn to the neon "Open" sign until a guy with tussled auburn hair and a peacoat that looks kind of like the one I have only cooler walks through my line of vision and I'm forced to jerk my head toward the sidewalk again. I cross the street and I'm on University and still walking quickly, passing more bars which, judging by the people standing around in front, aim for a clientele somewhere in their late-twenties, at the absolute youngest, with well paying jobs and I smirk at these neatly dressed yuppies, feeling my confidence rise for the first time this whole night, and I'm so satisfied thinking about those pathetic saps that I don't look down fast enough away from these two guys walking towards me so I quickly dodge to the right and hear one of them say "faggot" and the other one laugh. My face burns and I walk faster, speeding past everyone, desperate to get away from all these eyes, and I'm inhaling harder on the cigarette and practically choking smoke out. I feel dizzier than usual, even nauseated, and out of nowhere I gag, which for some reason helps snap me back into myself as I'm arriving at the corner of University and Sixth. A taxi is approaching fast but I run across the street anyway and when I get to the other side I'm on Broadway and gasping for breath and again I take out my cellphone and there's no word from Sam, thank god, but it's 7:55 and that makes my hands shake so I'm walking even faster, almost jogging now, past an outdoor falafel place, an art house, restaurants, more bars, and when I finally see the church across the street on Fourth my stomach jumps because I'm almost there. Trucks are passing while I'm on the corner of Broadway and Sixth and I'm trying to get myself to keep my eyes trained across the street but after a second or two, predictably, my head vibrates and I have to look away, at passing cars, the road, my feet, anything but the people in front of me. The crosswalk sign changes from lights in the pattern of a red hand to lights in the pattern of a white person and I'm rushing across the street, dodging the people walking towards me, and then I'm on Fourth and Sixth and walking fast past brownstones and the occasional apartment building, and then I'm walking past the monolithic steel entryway into Four Brothers and then I'm on the corner, waiting to cross one more street to get to Sam. The cigarette has burned down--I don't know when this happened but I just now realize I'm holdig an empty filter and I toss it aside before taking out my cellphone, which tells me it's 8:02, and I'm thinking "fuck, fuck" when the light changes and I'm across the street on Third and Sixth and I'm punching out a text message to Sam that says "Hey! I'm outside!" even though I'm not outside yet, I'm passing a RiteAid and then some restaurants but then, yeah, I'm outside Sam's building and I send the text message, almost panting. It's 8:05 and I immediately light a cigarette, leaning against the tall black gate outside Sam's dorm and trying to look cool, which for me just means looking calm. After about thirty seconds I get a text from Sam that says "Hey!! Sorry i'm late!! i'll be right down!!" which doesn't really make sense because he's not late, I am, but it makes me feel great because it means he likes me enough to take the blame for something that isn't his fault. I'm looking around the sidewalk in my general vicinity; a handful of boys and girls, some smoking cigarettes, some entering the building, some leaving, and I'm trying to think of what I'll say when Sam comes out but I don't have to think very long because he's here.

Sam looks fucking hot, period. He's wearing a tight turtleneck striped black and white that you can basically see his pecks through and tight, torn jeans and I know there's a bulge in his crotch but I resist the temptation to look there, obviously, instead looking at his gorgeous face and smiling. "Hey," I say, "how are you?"

"Hey Tad!" Sam practically squeals and rubs a hand over his abs, which turns me on. "It's great to see you," he says, stepping closer to me, and the combination of his blue eyes and his pale, perfect white skin is almost infectious. "It's great to see you too," I say, sheepishly, smiling, looking at the ground and then back at him, feeling something warm rushing through my face and body. Sam says, "Oh my god, I'm so sorry I'm late, my roommate was being a bitch and it took me like two hours to get ready." I say, "Don't worry about it," trying to sound nonchalant. "But um, fuck that. Yeah," Sam says, "we should get going. The show's at eight, right?" "Well, doors at eight, but yeah," I say back, "we should go." Then me and Sam are walking together, back to the corner of Third and Sixth, because we need to walk down two avenue blocks to get to the subway at Broadway and Sixth, and I'm walking in front of him kind of, leading the way, and I don't know if it's because Sam doesn't know the way or he's too nervous to walk next to me or he's just being nice, but I'm looking back at him every few seconds to catch a glimpse of what he is saying about his asshole roommate Jason, who is basically abusive, and I'm amazed by the fact that someone could be so cruel to someone so fragile and I feel like saying something like that to Sam but I don't know how to put it so I just allow myself to be amazed by his strange, ethereal beauty.

We're at the train station and I rush inside and swipe my MetroCard, Sam following me, and I scan the signs for a local train going downtown and when I see one I rush over there and down the stairs to the subway platform and only then do I look back for the first time since I entered the train station and see that Sam is right behind me. He isn't saying anything and he looks slightly annoyed about something but then he smiles again and says, "So who's the band we're going to see?" "I actually don't know," I say, smiling back, and that makes me feel reckless and cool. "Okay," Sam says, not smiling now. "Well, I'm sure it will be someone good." "Yeah," I say, "definitely." We're quiet then, standing next to each other, waiting for the subway, and we glance at each other roughly every thirty seconds and smile coyly, or at least I do, and then look away. The subway comes into the station and I approach the tracks, Sam following me. When the doors open I walk inside and quickly sit down at the last empty seat on a row of a empty seats and Sam sits down next to me. "This is gonna be so fun," Sam says, and I nod vigorously and say, "Yeah." An announcement to stand clear of the closing doors sounds and then the doors are closing with a hiss and Sam is saying, "Oh my god, thank you *so much* for getting me out of my dorm," and he puts a hand on my arm and I can barely breathe but, smiling uncontrollably, I muster a "No problem." "It's basically been Hell living with my roommate," Sam says, and I quickly interrupt and say "*Really?*," with what sounds to me like genuine concern and then Sam cuts back in and says, "Actually, let's not talk about that. I just need to forget about him. Let's just focus on having a really great time tonight," and he's smiling and so am I and I say, "Okay, yeah," and then we're quiet as the subway grinds down the tunnel.

The Bowery is the first stop and also where we have to get off for the Knitting Factory, so when the subway doors open I'm up and walking toward them, not looking back at Sam, just assuming he'll follow close behind, which I guess he does. We walk up the stairs to the subway exit like that and then we're on the street and smiling at each other again. Sam doesn't know where the Knitting Factory is so I focus all my attention on getting us there as fast as possible while

Sam says stuff about how cool it is that we have a black president and I agree with him enthusiastically. After about ten minutes of confusedly navigating through streets with names we're on Bowery and it's a relief to know that I know where we are.

"The club's right down there," I tell Sam, pointing.

"Oh, awesome! You're such a great guide," Sam says, catching up with me, and I do feel pretty great. We're walking down the street to the Knitting Factory and I barely even flinch when I make eye-contact with someone and we're outside the club before I know it, where some girl is talking about how her vagina is ashamed of Sarah Palin. Sam and I walk up the club's steps and Sam begins to chat up the bouncer while I just stand back smiling, barely smiling. Sam leans into me and says there's a ska band and a hip-hop thing going on inside and I say "Oh, cool!" and then we're inside the front door, which leads to the box office. Sam immediately starts talking to the guy at the box office and I'm standing back again, shooting glances at the two of them occasionally, watching Sam's blonde hair dance in front of his eyes in profile and feeling overwhelming love. I decide I should make my way into this conversation so I get closer to Sam, who turns to me once again and says that we can either see a ska band or open mic hip-hop. My immediate impulse is to go for the hip-hop thing, and not just because I'm wearing a tight green Def Jam hoodie from the '90s which I found at Metropolis, a store Sam introduced me to at the beginning of the semester. Sam, however, is insisting that we see ska, and for some reason the box office guy is recommending hip-hop. "I think you guys would like hip-hop more," the box office guy says with something like a wry smile and Sam keeps saying to him, "hmm, well, I don't know, I kind of want to check out ska. I know that's lame but I never really listen to ska and I'm with my friend here and..." and Sam speaks directly to me, saying "I don't know, what do you think?" and even though I know what I think I tell Sam, "Whatever you want is totally cool." After several minutes of me assuring Sam that I'm cool with whatever he wants to do and him for some reason talking to the box office guy he smiles at me and says, "Okay let's see that ska band." The box office guy tells Sam that tickets are ten bucks each at which point Sam takes out a wallet covered in a furry zebra pattern and says, "Oh no. I only have five dollars." I tell Sam it's totally cool, that I'll pay for us, and he apologizes and I say it's my fault for not telling him how much it would probably cost and I ask the box office guy if there's an ATM here and he points to one across the room which I now notice is incredibly small and terribly lit and as I'm walking over there Sam says to the box office guy, "Tad is such a sweet guy."

I swipe my card in the cash machine, withdraw forty bucks, and return to the table where the box office guy is sitting, handing him a twenty. He asks me and Sam for our hands and stamps them and tells us the ska thing is through the curtains behind him, which we walk through and the room is slightly smaller than the one we were just in and even darker and there's a band on the stage, which is really more of an elevated platform, playing what is, I guess, ska music. Noticing the bar at the left of the room I ask Sam if he wants a drink and he says he'd love one so we walk over there and sit down next to each other. We don't have wrist bands because we don't have fake Ids and when I try to order vodka the bartender notices this so instead I get a coke and Sam gets a glass of water. I'm staring at coke and Sam stands up and watches the band and every minute or so he leans in close to my face and says, "this is really great," and when he does that desire overwhelms everything but I don't know what to do with it. I can tell Sam is expecting something by the way he's looking at me, and I lean into him and he leans into me but then I stop and he pulls back and I realize one second too late that I was supposed to kiss him. Sam says he needs to go the bathroom and I say okay. He gets back after maybe thirty minutes, the band gets off stage and we leave.

Outside the Knitting Factory we see two guys, obviously older than us, obviously unwashed and even homeless-esque, sitting on the sidewalk. Sam goes over to them and begins talking to them. They're older than us, maybe in their twenties. Sam is asking this one guy, tall, with blond hair cut short, what he does, meaning, I'm thinking, in terms of school or a job. The tall guy answers that he has fun. The other guy sitting on the sidewalk, shorter, darker hair, a gray hoodie, says with a lisp that some people are sorry they're silly, but he's... "Silly you're sorry?" Sam guesses, and they all giggle except for me. The blond guy asks us, meaning Sam and me, what was going on in there, and Sam answers that it was some lame ska band, and don't get him wrong, he doesn't like ska, but...but the guy isn't paying attention, instead cracking open a tiny cellophane wrapped package to reveal white inside and snorting some of it before offering the rest to the other guy. I want some of whatever it is very badly, and when the blond guy asks Sam if he ever does Special K I have my answer, and Sam says he doesn't anymore, but he did snort meth once and the blond guy laughs out loud at this and turns to the guy with dark hair and says, "this kid is crazy," and the guy with dark hair isn't really paying attention, which calms me for some reason, and he just says "yeah," staring at the sidewalk. "I was on ecstasy the day we moved into the dorms," I offer, smiling limply at Sam, and Sam says "yeah" without looking at me and the blond guy turns from something he'd been staring at across the street to Sam and says, "so do you want to go

90

get saucy?" Sam asks, "What's get saucy?" and at this point an older guy, late-twenties at youngest, wearing rectangle glasses with thick black frames, shows up in front of us and asks the blond guy what the fuck he's doing. The blond guy looks at him, then looks at Sam, then points at the guy with glasses and says to Sam, "With him. Do you want to go get saucy with him?" Sam says, "Yeah!," and then he asks the blond guy again, "what's get saucy?" and the guy with glasses interjects and says to Sam, "To get drunk. He's asking you if you want to drink. I'm Neal by the way." Neal crouches down, shakes Sam's hand. Sam introduces himself, then as an afterthought nods in my direction and says, "This is my friend Tad." Neal bends down, shakes my hand, I say "nice to meet you," he stands up. "So, are you kids coming to Brooklyn with us? Me and this maniac?" He means the blond guy. Sam coyly says, "Yeah, let's go get saucy." "This guy owns the club we're going to," the blond guy slurs. "Whoa, are you serious?" Sam says. Neal is typing something into a Blackberry at this point and, without looking up, says to Sam, "Uh, yeah. We just need to find my girlfriend first..." Sam finally looks at me and says, "Oh, um, do you want to come?" I say, "No, I don't think so...I think I'm just going to back home..." and when I see the indifference with which Sam turns from me and then giggles at something the blond guy whispers to him I want to say, "Actually, yeah, I'll come," but I don't. The blond guy, Sam, and then me stand up, and Sam says, "well, I guess I'll see you later," and then he hugs me. I hug him back, lightly, and then Sam laughs and says, "I don't know why I did that. I hug all my friends." "Okay, I'll see you later," I say to Sam, and I lock eyes with him one last time. It feels like I'm pleading with him for some reason.

I take the subway back uptown and as I'm walking back to my dorm a homeless guy asks me for a cigarette, which

I give him. He thanks me, and when I'm halfway up the block he shouts after me, "Hey, do you want a blowjob?" I ignore him.

22.

It's Sunday afternoon and I'm lying on my bed. I'm high. My roommate is lying on his bed, also high. The movie we're watching is The Lord Of The Rings: The Return Of The King. I ask my roommate if he wants to smoke more. He says yes. We do.

23.

My name is Kyle Bern. My mother is Carol King. My father is Larry Bern. I have a brother and a sister. Their names are Ryan and Sarah. I'm from Summit, New Jersey. I wrote the book you just read. Right now Tom calls me from Delaware and tells me to meet him in five minutes. I'm in New York so I don't know what the fuck he's talking about, but only for a second, because I realize it's a Saturday and Tom is probably blitzed out of his mind on coke, or ecstasy, or who the fuck knows what else. I sigh in mock disgust, hoping Tom thinks I'm disapproving of his behavior, but really I'm just jealous because I've been kicking for months now while all my friends, everyone else around me, still gets to indulge in all the crazy drug binges they want. Come to think of it, that's probably a big part of why I wrote this book.

Tom's talking fast, saying something about us doing a bank heist, and I'm nodding involuntarily and saying "uh huh" but my thoughts are on Central Park and the dealer I'm supposed to meet there, not for me, of course, because I'm too *fucked*, naturally, to do drugs, to have fun, but for my roommate who will be paying me an extra ten bucks, a ten bucks I no longer know what to do with now that I've stopped doing drugs, to pick up for him, and even though I don't really care about the money I'm doing it anyway because I'm such a nice guy.

Tom's still babbling when I hang up on him, because I can tell this is going to take a while, and then I hit myself in the face with my cellphone a few times, just 'cause, and I whirl around and take a few deep breaths and then try to find the nearest subway. The idea of getting on a subway and making my way to Central Park to meet this guy, Ricky D, is giving me a minor panic attack and I have no idea how I'm going to handle it, but I put a cigarette in my mouth and light it and call Phil, because I know calling Greg is not an option right now and Phil will make me feel better.

Phil is extraordinary patient with me as I babble in high-pitched yelps about this and that, about how much pain I'm in and how much I hate being alive, but I can already tell he's bored and wants me off the phone so he can go back to sleep so I tell him "thanks" and hang up.

I'm 18 and I'm a freshman in college. I would tell you what college but that would probably be giving away too much, because I don't want you to find me, or know who I am, ever. It's a college in New York City, Manhattan, and that's all I'll say for now.

On the first day of college—the first day I moved in, actually, in late August, not the first day of classes—I was on half a tablet of the legal ecstasy I bought in Europe which was doing a fantastic job of quelling any anxiety I might have felt. I went through the motions of checking in, getting my room key, moving my shit into my room, and I looked at it all with a detached smugness, directed especially towards the insecurities of everyone around me and *especially* towards the smug fuckholes from L.A. with their bleached hair and smirking grins as they stood around the outskirts of the room during orientation, their bitches hanging off their arms and giggling, and it was so obvious and pathetic how much they were acting, trying to conceal their fears, that I wanted to fucking puke.

I'm the most genuine guy I know, and because of that I get put through a whole hell of a lot of shit.

But anyway, here I am now, cellphone in hand, somewhere at the west end of Union Square, and I need to catch that subway to Central Park to pick up from that guy. And just as I'm about to do this a gigantic object falls from the sky and crashes down in front of me.

24.

Kay is in in the studio in the basement at 12th Street. The fluorescent lighting makes the gigantic space seem like a place without time, which is exactly how Kay wants it to seem. She's standing over a table covered in sketches and paintings-in-progress. She's been awake for, she thinks, almost thirty-six hours. Eating is a lot easier than not eating. This is where her thoughts are looping, so it's time to take another Adderall. Which she does. Now she's looking at the Scottish guy with shoulder-length black hair way at the other end of the studio, by the exit, which is by the laundry room, which means kids, girls who spend an hour a day at the gym and keep a running tally of every carb in everything they eat, and Sam, that awkward asshole, could all possibly see her in here, which makes her start picking...but the Scottish guy, Greg, she thinks, double majoring in jazz and fine art, she thinks, is so fucking hot, if only she would go over there and talk to him. Instead she's glancing across the studio, hoping to catch his gaze, but he's fixated on a canvas on a stand next to a big black table, just like the table she's at. Kay is twirling her own obviously dyed black hair while she examines her drawing-to-be. It's a portrait of a gaunt woman screaming. Kay based the sketch on Kate Moss or maybe an old photo of herself in high school, she can't remember now. She adds some wavy lines to the cheekbones but she can't concentrate. The Adderall hasn't kicked in yet. Looking at the sketch, she knows she's good, she knows she's *better* than these shallow, talentless hipsters, and she really, *really* cares, which will always separate her from them and will get her a career that inspires her someday but right now this fucking Studio Art assignment--draw a portrait of a person conveying extreme emotion--is due at 8:00 tomorrow morning and she just...needs to...Kay is thinking about fucking the Scottish jazz major and she squeezes her thighs together but then Sam, fucking Sam that miserable skinny piece of shit is in her thoughts now and everything's ruined. She's scratching her face now, digging fingernails into skin, unconscious of what she is doing but aware of the smooth-ish feeling of flesh, hunched over her portrait, head in hands, and she can't remember the last time she ate or what time it is and she thinks about the snack machine upstairs and then she feels blood.

25.

You think about the first day of freshman orientation, how you were on ecstasy, and it felt exciting just to be around so many living human bodies and at President Terry's welcoming speech you sat next to a guy with a shaved head wearing a t-shirt with neon green writing on it and a watch that looked like it came from a cereal box in the '90s and you kept looking at him, trying to decide if he was a douchebag and then whether or not you would fuck him, and you missed part of Terry's speech, which everyone laughed and clapped for, including the guy sitting next to you, and you stared straight at the wobbly gray-haired man at the podium when the kid sitting next to you, still giggling, leaned over and stared right at you, a grin plastered to his face, and he kind of whispered, "Never forget." Stoned, you replied, "Never forget...what?" The kid looked at the stage and started laughing harder, along with the audience, and then he pulled himself back into you and kind of whispered, "Never forget that they don't give a fuck about you."

26.

And it was like the time in high school AP English class when Emily's stomach was growling and she looked up from her desk and said to no one, "my stomach," smiling meekly, so no one would think it was her gastrointestinal system at work boiling something up for her ass, but of course no one gave a shit. But then again, maybe someone did. And also, then again, maybe it wasn't like that at all.